Suddenly the door opened. From the light, Mickie could see that it wouldn't be hard at all. Reno came out with only the girl. As he approached the car, the three men stepped out. The guns in their hands gave warning. The girl screamed and Reno wished for the last time that he had his hands on a gun. It was over that quick. All three men fired, the girl dropped before Reno did, but when they fell Johnnie-Bee made sure they were dead. He walked over to both bodies and shot them in the head.

MAR 2017

SF

Holloway House Originals by Donald Goines

DOPEFIEND
WHORESON
BLACK GANGSTER
STREET PLAYERS
WHITE MAN'S JUSTICE,
    BLACK MAN'S GRIEF
BLACK GIRL LOST
CRIME PARTNERS
CRY REVENGE
DADDY COOL
DEATH LIST
ELDORADO RED
INNER CITY HOODLUM
KENYATTA'S ESCAPE
KENYATTA'S LAST HIT
NEVER DIE ALONE
SWAMP MAN

Special preview of *Inner City Hoodlum*—page 193

ELDORADO RED

RED

Donald Goines

www.kensingtonbooks.com

DEDICATED TO

Marie and Joan Goines. Because both of my sisters believed in my writing ability when I had just about given up hope of ever being published.

Donald Goines

1

SHIRLEY BOOTH HANDLED the small compact car as if it was a toy. She drove like a man. Every now and then she'd glance at the younger woman sitting next to her.

"Dolores, do you think you'll ever learn this numbers route? It's so damn spread out, you know. That's the problem. Sometimes I wonder if it's even worth it, running all over the damn place picking up each customer's play."

"I've just about got it down pat now, Shirley," Dolores answered quickly. "It's just the small stops like the one we're going to now that get me mixed up. Too many damn small stops, if you ask me,"

Dolores stated sharply as she glanced over at the older woman.

As the women became silent Dolores wondered idly why Shirley had never become bigger in Eldorado's numbers outfit. She had been with Eldorado Red ever since he'd first started out back in the fifties. From what she'd heard people say, Shirley used to be a fine bitch in her prime, before she allowed herself to become so heavy, and yet Shirley still had a shape. She wasn't what you'd call real fat, but she was big. She wore expensive clothes that made her look better than what another woman her size would look like in cheaper clothes.

Shirley turned on the freeway and drove over to the west side. She came up on Grand Boulevard and made a right turn at Ford's Hospital. At the first side street she made another right. She parked in front of a dilapidated house that sat back from the street. It was a small house that had once been painted white, but now from neglect the paint was peeling and it looked as if no one had lived in it for years.

As the two women walked up the long pathway leading to the front door, they both noticed someone watching them from one of the front windows.

"Goddamn it!" Shirley exclaimed loudly. "This damn place really gives me the creeps. Every time I have to pick up here I hate it. I'll be damn glad to give this route to you."

Dolores gestured at the long weeds that had taken the place of the grass. "Well, it does look like a jungle out here, but I would think a lawnmower would take care of that little problem."

"Honey," Shirley began, "it's not the grass that I'm talking about. Wait until you get inside the house. It will make the outside look like heaven, plus the fact that you have to put up with both those old bitches inside. Shit, a nuthouse would be a better resting place for them than here."

Before she could knock on the front door, it opened. As they started to go inside, Dolores stated quietly, "You're too cold, Shirley. One day we'll…." The sight of the old woman standing behind the door stopped Dolores' flow of words. Dolores stared at the old woman in surprise. She looked as if she wasn't a day under one hundred. Her skin was wrinkled like nothing she'd ever seen before. But the real shock was the eyes staring out of the black face at her. There was a gleam in them that spoke of madness.

"Lordie, lordie, lordie," the woman shouted at them like a parrot, "come on in, come on in." She held the door only halfway open so that the women had to squeeze past her.

As Shirley entered, she wondered for the thousandth time why Eldorado Red continued to carry the women. It was true that when the two sisters' brother was alive it had been a good stop, but he had died over five years ago, and since then the place had fallen off until it really wasn't worth the trouble for the field worker to stop there. It was just too small. Sometimes the sisters didn't have fifty dollars for their day's take, but she knew if she had brought the matter up to Red he'd just say every little bit counts.

   This was the first time Shirley had brought Dolores
to this stop. She glanced out of the corner of her eye
to see how the slim, brown-skinned young woman was
taking it. It was really a change from the other homes
they went to. There was a look of total surprise and
fright on Dolores' face at the sight of the horde of
roaches running wild on the walls of the front room.
   "Where the hell is Auntie Dee?" Shirley asked
sharply. She didn't want to stay in the house for any
length of time if it could be avoided. The roaches did-
n't frighten Shirley, but she didn't like the thought of
one of them falling on her. It made her flesh crawl.
   "Auntie Dee is the one who picks up the numbers
in the neighborhood," Shirley explained to Dolores.
"She takes care of all the work. This poor thing here
ain't too much help, she don't understand too much
other than the Bible. She'll talk you to death about
that, but nothing else."
   "Have a seat, have a seat," the old woman yelled
in a shrill voice, waving the women towards a dilapidated couch that was covered by a sheet and a blanket.
   Before Shirley could warn her, Dolores started to
sit down. A mouse ran from under the couch. Dolores
screamed and jumped on top of the couch. There was
no way Shirley could stop the flow of laughter that
was taking control of her. She bent over and laughed
until tears rolled down her face.
   Dolores never took her eyes off the mouse. She
watched the rodent go under the huge, old-fashioned
china cabinet that stood against the wall.

"Little Jesus, little Jesus," the old woman scolded as she banged on the china cabinet. "You bad thing you, scaring the woman like that."

"Now, now, Auntie," Shirley interrupted, "that ain't necessary you takin' on like that. It was my fault for not telling Dolores that you kept a few pet mice and rats around."

At the mention of rats, Dolores' eyebrows shot up and she glanced around nervously. She started to say something but the sound of a harsh voice coming from behind a curtain leading into the kitchen stopped her.

"Ya'll have to keep that fuss down out there if you expect me to ever finish writin' up these here figures."

"Is that you, Auntie Dee?" Shirley asked, knowing all along it was the woman she was looking for.

"Of course it is, child. Who'd you expect it to be? Maybe Miss World or somebody like that?" the woman behind the curtain yelled sharply.

Before Shirley could stop her, Dolores was up and heading for the kitchen. Possibly because of her fear of rats, she didn't wait for Shirley to lead the way. Shirley followed the younger woman even though she had never gone any farther than the front room. Her curiosity was aroused.

The elderly woman sitting at the kitchen table looked up in surprise as the two women came barging in. But the person who was really surprised was Dolores as she stopped and stared open-mouthed at the old woman in front of her. She was utterly unlike any woman Dolores had ever seen. The impact of her presence was almost tactile in the silence that greeted their unwelcome entry. The old woman was as black as her sister. Neither woman had that rich nightshade velvety blackness that had its own sable beauty. Instead, the woman sitting in front of them had a gray-black shade with a deeply purple tinge about her lips. Her face was a mass of wrinkles that made her seem immensely old. But her eyes were the feature that held them. There was an evil glare in the pinpoint pupils—an undeniable quality of evil that could not be hidden.

"Well?" the old woman asked sharply in that husky voice that seemed to come from the emptiness of a deep well.

This was not the first time Shirley had met Auntie Dee. Ever since the death of her brother, Auntie Dee had been handling the numbers route, so Shirley was acquainted with the woman. But for some reason, the sight of Auntie Dee always gave Shirley a sense of fear. The old woman had never done anything to her, but the feeling was there just the same.

"Ya'll could have waited just as well in the front room for me to finish addin' up these here figures instead of running all over my house this-ways," Auntie Dee stated harshly.

Shirley had no doubt that the woman could see she was blushing. For something to do, Shirley fumbled around in her purse and found her eyeglasses.

"Sorry about this," Dolores spoke up loudly. "It's my fault we came barging in your kitchen. I heard your voice and just didn't think. We're running late today, so I just wasn't thinking."

"This goin' be my new pick-up girl?" Auntie Dee asked sharply, writing out numbers on a slip of paper.

"Yes, I'm the person who'll be stopping to pick up your stuff every day," Dolores replied. Suddenly she noticed something over the stove on the wall. It looked as if the wall was alive. It moved. She shook her head and squinted at the wall again, and again it seemed to move.

Auntie Dee finished writing out her figures, folded up the paper and stuck it in an envelope which held some other slips. "It seems as if my route's gettin' smaller every day," Auntie Dee offered as an excuse as she held out the envelope. "There ain't but twenty-eight dollars inside, but things goin' pick up. Ya just have a little patience with me." There was a slight hint of pleading in her voice. The few extra dollars they made off the numbers route probably helped the women pay off many of their bills.

Dolores didn't notice the envelope being offered to her. She was too busy trying to see what was on the back wall of the kitchen. Shirley reached over and took the envelope from Auntie Dee's hand.

After glancing at the figures on the outside of the package, Shirley shook her head. "I don't know, Auntie Dee, it's gettin' awful small. You had better try and pick up some of your old business. Why, we used to pick up as high as two hundred dollars a day through the week here. This kind of take," Shirley shook the envelope, "this ain't worth the price it cost us to pay Dolores here to come pick up."

"Ouch, Goddamn it!" Shirley cursed loudly as

Dolores backed up on her foot. "Watch what the hell you're doing."

Dolores didn't even hear her in her haste to get out of the kitchen. Shirley grabbed her arm and held her tightly. "What the hell's wrong with you?"

For a minute Dolores couldn't speak, she only pointed. "On the wall, over the stove. Is it what I think it is?" she finally managed to say.

As Shirley adjusted her glasses on her nose, Auntie Dee spoke up. "Shit!" she exclaimed loudly. "Where's that child been living? She ain't never seen a few roaches before?"

By now, Shirley could make out the black mass of caked up roaches. There were so many of them that it seemed as if the wall was alive. They seemed to move in unison. There were so many of them that you could take a piece of cardboard and scrape them off without reaching the wall underneath. Roaches living on top of roaches. The smaller ones on the bottom had been crushed to death by the larger ones on top. It seemed to Shirley that the wall held more roaches than all the roaches she had ever seen in her life. Putting together every roach-infested house she had ever been in, none of them had ever come close to showing such a display of filth.

The fear that Dolores felt only added fuel to Shirley's own terror. Ordinarily the sight of a few roaches wouldn't have disturbed either woman. But so many at one time was a terrifying sight.

"My God," Shirley murmured as she backed out of the kitchen with Dolores clutching her arms. And it was a good thing the women backed out, because over the doorway was another mass of roaches. As they tumbled through the doorway, the footsteps jarred a few of the roaches loose and they fell down on the women.

"Oh, ooooh shitttt! Goddamn it!" Dolores screamed as she brushed the roaches off her arm.

Shirley thought that the creatures had fallen in her hair. She reached up and snatched the expensive wig off her head. She shook it out as she fled from the house.

Auntie Dee followed the women out of the house and stopped on the porch. She stared after the running women in shock. "Why, I never," she began, then shook her head. She turned and glanced at her sister who stood in the doorway holding the envelope that Shirley had dropped.

"Can you believe grown women could act like that at the sight of a few roaches? I do declare, women ain't women no damn more." Then it dawned on her what her sister was holding. She grabbed the envelope out of her sister's hand and rushed down the narrow sidewalk as fast as her skinny legs would allow, waving the envelope.

"Hold up there, gal, you done run off and left everything," she screamed as she ran up to the car.

Shirley sat behind the steering wheel crying hysterical tears as she held her wig. Neither woman had gotten complete control of themselves yet. "My God," Shirley murmured softly, "the sight of them things made my flesh crawl. I still feel as if I've got the fuckin' things all over me."

Auntie Dee banged on the window. "Here, child, ya done run out and left the figures. I don't know what got into you girls, acting like that."

For a minute Dolores just stared at the woman peering in at them. She couldn't quite understand what Auntie Dee was saying. It was more her nerves than anything else that caused laughter to build up inside her. It was like a relief valve, releasing the tension that had been built up inside. Dolores laughed so hard that tears ran down her cheeks, while Auntie Dee stood outside the car banging on the window waving the policy slips wildly.

Shirley knew she should do something, but for the moment her brain locked on her. She couldn't get her thoughts together. The wild laughing of Dolores didn't help matters either. She started the motor so that she could let the window down and receive the package that Auntie Dee kept waving so crazily.

The sound of the motor starting put Auntie Dee in a frenzy. "Just a minute," Shirley yelled as she let the window down.

None of the women had noticed the police car that had pulled up beside them. They were all too occupied to pay any attention to what was going on outside. Shirley was reaching out for the envelope that contained the numbers when the policeman knocked on her window.

As Shirley glanced over her shoulder and saw the policeman knocking, the first thing that crossed her mind was that she was busted. There was no doubt

about it. The policemen had heard Auntie Dee screaming about the numbers inside the envelope.

One quick glance at the policemen brought Dolores
back to reality. She realized that she had a pocketbook
full of numbers. The only thing she didn't realize was
that they were already busted. She had no way of
knowing that the officers had watched most of the
proceedings. What they hadn't witnessed themselves
they could just about fill in from the shouting Auntie
Dee had been doing. There wasn't the slightest doubt
in their minds as to what the envelope held.

Shirley tried to straighten up. She knew that they
were on their way downtown and that there was no
reason for her to look like a tramp. She began to put
the wig back on.

2

CHARLES WILLIAMS STOOD in the bathroom and admired his physique. "Not bad," he said as he patted his growing stomach. Charles stood over six foot two barefoot. His physique wasn't anything a young man in his teens or early twenties would have been proud of, but for a man forty years old, it was above average. His stomach was too fat, but other than that, he could justly say he was in good shape. He still possessed all of his teeth, bragging that he had never even had a toothache. He wore his hair cut close in a neat natural that was graying at the edges.

Charles stepped on the bathroom scale and the needle went up to two hundred and ten pounds. Charles grinned as he got down and did ten quick pushups. "Not bad," he said again, not in the least out of breath. "For an old man, I'd say, Eldorado Red, you're in the best of health."

"Were you talking to me, Red?" his latest young girl asked from the bedroom.

Eldorado Red took one last look in the full-length mirror before walking out of the bathroom. He pranced around the bed. The young, attractive black girl was stretched out on the lush spread.

"Tina," he said in that loud voice of his, "I'd say you are about one of the luckiest bitches in this cold old world we live in."

Tina tried to frown. "You know I don't like that word, Red. I ain't nobody's bitch, and I don't like to be called one either."

Red stopped his prancing and glanced down at her. "Hey, baby, how many times do I have to tell you that bitch is a term of endearment? It depends on what tone of voice the person uses. Now, when I spoke of it a minute ago, I was really only using it as a figure of speech. If you found something depraved about the word, honey, it's in your own little mind."

For a minute Tina just stared up at him, then she sat up on the edge of the bed. "There you go again, 'Rado Red, using them words. When you start talking like that, you make everything seem right."

Charles Williams, better known by his friends as Eldorado Red, just smiled a cold, bitter smile. It was the smile of a man who had seen just about everything there is to see. "Tina, you are one lucky girl.

For one thing, you don't think too much. At least I don't believe you do anyway. All you're concerned about is a pretty dress and learning the latest dance steps."

The irony in his voice was missed by Tina. "You goin' let me go shopping today?" she asked greedily.

Just as quickly as his good mood had come, it vanished. Tina watched the tall, light-skinned man stride over to the dresser and pick up his pants. He slipped them on quickly, reached in the pocket and counted his money.

"Here, honey," he said as he peeled off a hundred dollars and tossed it on the bed. "When you finish shopping, rent you a room at a motel downtown somewhere. That way you'll be closer to the stores you like so well."

It took a second for Tina to realize it, but she had somehow managed to get on the wrong side of him. Eldorado was mad and she couldn't understand why. "Honey, you're not angry with me, are you?" she inquired sweetly.

"Angry! Why, baby, what could you possibly do to make me lose my cool?" he asked, smiling at her. Had she paid closer attention, she would have noticed that the smile didn't quite reach his eyes. They remained a misty gray—cold and bleak.

"Well then, daddy, ain't no sense me wasting no good money on no old motel room. Besides, I hate to sleep alone. I'll just do my shopping and catch a cab back here."

"No, I'm afraid you won't do that either," Eldorado

answered quietly. "When you leave, you'll take all the clothes you've been buying the past week with you." Before she could say anything, he went on. "I mean it, Tina, I don't like for a bitch to think she's playing on me. I've been kind to you all this week, honey, giving you money to go shopping, but I don't like for a bitch to try and hustle me." He waved her reply down. "Don't say it, it will only make matters worse, Tina. Yes, you did try and hustle me. Even if you don't have the sense to realize it, you did try. Every fuckin' day this week, I've given you better than a hundred dollars each day. As long as you didn't ask for it, it was all right, but today, honey, you let the cat out of the bag. So you take that little money and make the best of it."

She ran over to the man and put her arms around his waist. "Oh, daddy, I know it must be more than that to it. Did Buddy say something to you? 'Cause if he did, he was lying. I ain't had nothing to do with your son, even though he's been hittin' on me ever since I got here."

The coldness in his eyes became chilling as he stared down at the woman with her head on his chest. "Tina, I haven't even talked to my son, so don't say anything you might regret. If he's been hittin' on you, I don't want to know nothing about it."

Eldorado pushed the woman away from him. The thought that his son would stoop to hit on one of the chippies that he brought home filled him with a rage. He had been very good to the boy ever since Buddy had left his mother's home six months ago and moved in with him. He had tried to give Buddy everything a young boy of eighteen could want—his own car and clothes that any boy would be proud of. Anything Buddy wanted, all he had to do was ask for it. The very thought of his own son going behind his back after one of the cheap bitches that Eldorado brought home was almost unbearable. He didn't even want to look at the girl in front of him. Of course she was young enough to be his daughter, but that wasn't the point. He hated betrayal on any level. And the thought of his own son attempting to go behind his back was disgusting.

"Get out!" he ordered harshly. "Take your shit and get the fuck out of my sight, Tina. I mean it! I want you out of here as soon as goddamn possible!"

Tina took one look at his face and decided to follow his orders. He might change his mind and decide to take back the clothes he had bought for her. The thought of that happening filled her with more fear than the thought of a beating. She rushed around the room gathering up her stuff. Eldorado turned away from her and left the bedroom.

He walked out into his luxurious living room and sat down. Red reached over and tapped a switch on the couch and music came flowing out of the walls. The sound was everywhere. His glance went around his beautiful, eighty-thousand dollar home. It hadn't always been like this. It had taken hard work to get where he was. That was one reason why the thought of his son's betrayal hurt so much. He had been planning on teaching Buddy everything about his organi-

zation there was to know, so that one day he could
just turn it all over to his only son. Eldorado Red
laughed harshly. It wasn't a very pleasant sound coming from him. It carried the bitterness that he felt so
deep down. Nothing had ever been given to him. He'd
have been happy if his dad had given him a pair of
shoes when he came up, let alone a new sports car
and all the damn clothes a kid could want.

The years slipped past as he sat there and he
remembered the cold days he had spent walking from
house to house picking up each player's number personally and how he had had to turn in all the plays
for over a dollar to another, bigger numbers outfit
because his small bankroll couldn't stand a hit for over
five hundred dollars. All the dime and two-bit plays
were his meat at the time, but the day finally came
when he could take the chance and hold onto some
of the dollar bets. He'd been lucky then because
nobody ever hit on him for over fifty cents.

What had made his name good was the way he paid
off. Whenever someone did hit, whether it was for
pennies, dimes or fifty cents, he'd personally make
sure they got their money the first thing in the morning. As soon as he was sure the number wouldn't be
changed, he'd be there with their money. His reputa-
tion for paying off quickly spread, so that soon new
customers were asking for him.

Eldorado Red's numbers route grew from a small
hundred-dollar-a-day route up to where he was picking up five hundred dollars a day. Then he had started hiring the girls to work for him. Shirley had been

one of the first. He had given her his own personal route while he started to build up another one from the new customers coming in. It had been slow, but it had finally paid off.

Tina came out of the bedroom carrying her suitcase. "Eldorado, honey, I don't see why we should have to end up like this. I mean, we was getting along so fine, then all of a sudden we fall out. I don't really understand yet; what happened?"

Red just stared at her. "Did you call you a cab?"

When she said that she had, he added, "I think it would be best if you went out on the porch and waited on it, Tina."

Before she could say anything, they heard a horn blowing. "That's probably your cab now," Eldorado said coldly.

Tina gathered up her belongings. She started to say something to him, but his face was set in such hard lines that she changed her mind.

Red watched her walk out of his home and, he hoped, out of his life. He glanced at his watch. It was getting time to go over to his drop-off house and find out if everybody came in off their routes. He didn't anticipate any problems; he just received personal happiness from being around the receiving house when all the numbers came in. It filled him with pride to see all the money stacked up on the table. Red was a self-educated man so he took a lot of pride in his accomplishment. To know that he was the creator of his own organization, one that took in from five to ten thousand dollars every day, gave him much pleasure. Eldorado Red knew it wasn't what you would call a big outfit, but it was big enough.

Red walked to the window and watched the woman get in the cab. Good, that was one problem off his back. It would be a damn long time before he'd allow another bitch to move into his house, he told himself harshly. That was a mistake he could do without. Eldorado went back into the bedroom and finished dressing. Dressed in neat slacks and matching dark blue shirt, he checked the expensive watch on his arm to make sure he had enough time, then locked the front door behind him as he left. The bright red Eldorado Cadillac sat inside the garage. Eldorado had once taken pride in buying a new Cadillac every year. But now the cars were just another form of transportation.

That was the way life went, he rationalized. Things that you used to take pleasure in became common, unexciting and ordinary affairs. Maybe he was getting old; that could be one reason why nothing seemed like it used to be. At one time he would have never gotten mad at Tina, understanding that it was just a young girl's greed. Any black girl that had never had anything would have been carried away with what he had to offer. A beautiful home, a swimming pool in the backyard, and other things that he took for granted were exciting to a girl like Tina. But people like Buddy were different. Buddy took everything for granted, as if it were his due. Maybe that was the problem. He had never sat Buddy down and explained that no one owed Buddy or his mother anything.

Especially that bitch he called mother, Vera. A tall, brown-skinned woman who was too attractive for her own good. A woman who used her beauty for a tool to bend other people to her will.

Eldorado Red backed the long Cadillac out of the driveway. He didn't bother to glance back at the beautiful ranch-type home he was leaving. The well-kept lawn and the beautifully trimmed hedge that spoke of money were things that he had worked a lifetime to achieve. It didn't cross his mind that there was a possibility he might end up losing everything he had worked so hard to gain. But even at that moment, incidents were working that would push him to the wall. People were scheming to overthrow his small organization, and even as he drove slowly toward town, other people were riding, carrying guns. Their one motive was to relieve Eldorado Red of some of that hard cash they knew he had.

3

THE FOUR MEN RIDING in the car laughed and talked louder than was necessary. Wine bottles passed from the back to the front with frequency as they neared their destination.

"Goddamn, Buddy, you're sure now it ain't but five women and two men in this joint, man?" a fat, dark-complexioned young man asked for the tenth time.

Buddy, a tall, light-complexioned Negro, twisted around in his seat in the front of the car and glanced back at the man. "Listen, Tubby, my man, I ain't wasting my time settin' this shit up for nothing. When I say it ain't but so many people in one of these joints, I know what I'm talking about. If you're scared shit-

less, man, just say so. If you want out, it's damn near
too late for that. We done went over this shit for a
month gettin' the right people together and everything,
so now it's D-Day."

The men fell silent in the car while Tubby wiped
the sweat from his brow. He didn't want the rest of
the guys to know that he was frightened. Eldorado
Red wasn't no punk, no matter what Buddy said.
Tubby had been around for a long time and he knew
about a few of the things Eldorado Red had done when
he was climbing to the top of his field.

"Naw, man, I ain't scared; it's just that I'm thinkin'
close on this thing, man. It just seems as if it's too
easy. I mean, a guy like your old man just don't take
chances, Buddy. It's too pat," Tubby answered
doggedly.

Buddy gave him his practiced sneer. "My old man
is a punk, man. He don't know nothin' but how to
smell under some funky young bitch's dress. That's
all he's got on his mind, man, pussy. That's it, pussy,"
he repeated harshly as he thought about Tina and how
the fine young bitch had turned her back on him. How
the bitch could prefer his father to him, Buddy would
never understand. It hurt his pride.

Samson, a husky, brown-skinned brother, took his
eyes off the street for a moment to glance at Buddy.
"Your old man may be a lot of things, Buddy, but he
ain't no punk, man," Samson stated loudly. Whenever
he spoke the rest of the men paid attention because
Samson was the kind of man you respected. He wasn't
tall, but he was built wide, standing about five foot

nine with huge shoulders. His muscles seemed to move on their own when he walked.

"Yeah, man," Buddy replied coldly, "I done heard all that shit about how my old man handled the dagos when they tried moving in on his numbers outfit." He didn't try to conceal the contempt in his voice as he continued. "To listen to you guys tell it, my old man is one ball of fire. Yes siree, he's just too goddamn much."

The silence that invaded the car was heavy. Each man looked away from his neighbor as if he didn't want the man next to him to see the uneasiness that was all too apparent.

"Mother fuck-it," Samson stated coldly. "If you want to fool yourself, Buddy, that's all right with me, but don't think I'm buying that shit. Ain't no fools in this car, man. Each and every one of us know just what we're gettin' into. Your old man might not do nothing to you about knockin' off one of his joints, but he'll bury one of our black asses if he ever gets wind of it being us who knocks off this pickup."

"Amen to that!" Danny, a slim, jet-black drug addict, stated. "It ain't no motherfuckin' doubt about it going any other way than that way, man. When we fuck over Eldorado's shit, the dues are going to be mean for whatever nigger gets his nuts caught in the sand. Me, I ain't worried 'cause I'm pullin' up for the Big Apple tonight, right after we split up the cash."

"You been going to the Big Apple ever since I met you, Danny," Buddy replied harshly. "The furthest you goin' get with your money, man, is the nearest dope house."

"Dig this, my man," Danny began, "if I don't never get to New York it ain't nobody's motherfuckin' concern but mine. Maybe I find my thing in talkin' about going to the Big Apple. But whether or not I go is still my business and not yours, my man. So don't be so quick in calling me a lie, 'cause you don't know me that well, man, and I really don't like for nobody to call me a lie."

The slim drug addict hadn't raised his voice, but the message was there loud and clear. Danny was a dangerous man, regardless of his size. Just how dangerous he was was well known by everybody except Buddy. Buddy was fairly new to the crowd. He had been with them long enough for them to have confidence in him. For the past three years, off and on, whenever Buddy came over for the summer to visit with Eldorado Red, he ended up running with the three men in the car. But Danny's friendship with Samson and Tubby dated back to their childhood days when they went to school together.

Something seemed to warn Buddy because he fell silent, letting the matter drop. But he didn't fear Danny. To him, Danny was just a dumb-ass drug addict, one he would squash if the small man ever got in his way. Instead of arguing, he let his mind wander. He thought about his mother and brother and sisters back in the cold-water flat in Chicago. Four women and one boy fifteen years old crowded together in one filthy four-room apartment. The very thought of it made his jaw tighten in anger. All that room that no one used at Eldorado's house, yet his brother and sisters and mother had to make use of a rat-infested building. He was the oldest of the children, and the only child his mother bore for Eldorado Red, but he still held his father guilty of his mother's problem. His mother had run out on Red when Buddy was only a year old, choosing a pimp with a new Cadillac and going to Chicago. One Christmas five years later she had called and given Red her address so that he could send some money for the child. After that, every month until the boy was grown, Eldorado Red had sent one hundred dollars to Chicago. If Buddy had asked, Red could have shown him money order stubs dating back fifteen years. But Buddy never asked; he enjoyed nourishing his hatred.

The sight of a police cruiser put all of the men inside the car on alert. Where before the men had been slumped over and relaxed, now they were tense. Nobody glanced over at the police car as they pulled up beside it.

"You goin' pass them?" Tubby asked excitedly as they drew up next to the policemen. Samson didn't bother to answer. As the policemen glanced over at the passing car, Samson pretended to be laughing then made a gesture with his hand as he talked. It was all play acting for the benefit of the policemen.

"What are the bastards doing now, huh?" Danny asked from the backseat.

"Just be cool, man, just be cool. The motherfuckin' pigs are still behind us, so just take it easy. I don't think the cocksuckers have made up their cotton-pickin' minds whether or not to fuck with us." It was the same feeling that all black men had when they saw the police. Whether or not they had done anything didn't make any difference. They were black and that was enough. It meant it was open season on them. At any time they could be stopped and made to get out on the sidewalk with their hands in the air while the car was searched.

This time they were dirty. There were three guns in the car and that meant a prison term for each man if the police decided to stop them and search the automobile.

"Man, if they look like they want to fuck with us, let's make a run for it. Maybe if you can gain a block on them," Danny stated in a matter-of-fact voice, "we'll have time to throw these pistols out."

Samson glanced in his mirror. "They're stickin' pretty damn close to our bumper, but if it looks like they've decided to fuck with us, I'll do what I can. Ain't no sense in layin' down like a wet duck."

"Bust a cap at them motherfuckers," Buddy said, his voice shaking. "I don't want to go to no joint on no bullshit. If we blast at their ass, maybe we can get away."

"That's dead, baby. That's the coldest shit in town. The last thing in the world we want is a gunfight with the police." Samson looked sharply at Buddy. "Are you out of your fuckin' mind? We ain't got no reason to hold court. Even if they stop us, everybody ain't got to fall. So they find some fuckin' guns in the car. They don't have to belong to everybody. I'll ride the beef out first before I'd let everybody fall on the same motherfuckin' charge."

Buddy wiped the sweat off his brow. "Okay, my man," he said with a smile. "Just remember your words. If we get uptight I hope you remember everything you just said." He hesitated for a second, then added, "I can dig where you're coming from, though. It don't take everybody to do one bit."

As Samson glanced at him sharply, Buddy continued. "As far as I'm concerned, I don't know nothing about no guns. All of them are still in the glove compartment, ain't they?"

Danny laughed bitterly. "You're one cold motherfucker, Buddy. I wouldn't trust you in a shithouse with a muzzle on."

"What the fuck do you mean by that?" Buddy asked quickly. "If you got something on your mind, man, come on out with it!"

Suddenly Samson let out a breath of relief. "The motherfuckers turned off. They must have got a call or something. I'd have bet a twenty-dollar bill against a bucket of shit that they were going to fuck with us. It just goes to show, you can't never tell."

The men relaxed and joked back and forth the rest of the way. It was as if the police car had taken all the tension out of the robbery. Now they were ready. Samson parked the car a few doors down from the apartment building they were to enter.

As they sat in the car waiting for the delivery man to arrive, Buddy scanned the street searching for that Eldorado that he knew so well. He let out a sigh of relief when he didn't see the car. If the other men knew that there was a chance of Eldorado Red showing up, they'd call the job off. Buddy prayed under his breath that this was one of the days that Red would be late showing up or wouldn't bother to stop by.

The sudden appearance of a catering truck brought the men up in their seats. "Is that the one that delivers the food?" Danny asked from the back.

"More than likely that's it," Buddy replied. "Like I said, they use a different delivery service just about every day. That way the drivers of the trucks don't get any ideas."

"You better get ready, Danny," Samson ordered as he reached over and opened up the glove compartment. He quickly removed the guns and passed them out. "Buddy, you go with Tubby and bring back the driver. After that, you can sit the rest of the caper out just watching him."

For a brief second Buddy hesitated. He had hoped that he wouldn't have any reason to put a gun in his hand. That way, if something happened, he could always play on the fact that he hadn't used a gun. Now, if he followed Samson's order, he would be involved no matter what happened. The delivery man would never forget him, he was sure of that.

His mind worked overtime trying to come up with an excuse, but he couldn't find one that was usable. It wasn't that he was scared, but Buddy just didn't want to get involved if it was possible for him not to.

"Well, my man, what the fuck are you going to do? Let the man get away?" Samson asked sharply.

For an answer, Buddy opened up the car door and got out, followed closely by Tubby. The two men approached the driver of the truck quickly. "All right, mister, don't breathe too hard if you know what's good for you," Buddy said as he stuck the gun into the ribs of the truck driver.

The driver, a heavyset Negro, started to raise his hands. "Just take it easy, kid," he said. "I ain't got enough money on me to die for. You can have every fuckin' thing you see. This is just a job to me; I don't owe the company enough to lose my life over."

"Just keep your hands down then," Tubby ordered from the other side of the man. "You don't give us no trouble and we won't give you none. Just follow directions like you got good sense, my man." Tubby's voice was low, but there was no mistaking the determination behind the orders.

"We don't want your money, man, we just want to deliver those dinners for you, that's all," Buddy stated, then added, "Now, I want you to walk with us back to that car down the street. Just act normal, you know, as if we were old friends."

Before Buddy finished instructing the man, Tubby had taken the frightened man's arm and led him down the sidewalk. As they approached the car, the door opened and Danny got out, dressed in a delivery man's outfit. The catering man took one glance at Danny then quickly glanced around at the two men walking beside him. "I mean, I know it ain't none of my business, but what's going on?" he asked quietly.

"The less you know, the better off you'll be,"

Buddy stated as he shifted the two dinners he had picked up off the tailgate of the catering truck. He held the well-wrapped meals out to Danny. "Here's your calling card, baby," he stated as Danny took the food from him.

The men stood beside the car until Samson came around the car to the sidewalk. He opened up the car door and held it for the driver to get in. "You just sit down and relax, mister. Ain't nobody goin' hurt you if you just follow orders. We ain't got no misunderstanding with you, so just be cool. We'll let you go in a few minutes if you just be cool."

Buddy directed the man to the backseat, then climbed in with him after glancing up and down the street one more time, praying that his father hadn't pulled up. Buddy held the gun in his lap, not aiming it directly at the hostage.

"We're going to get along just fine, ain't we, brother?" Buddy asked as his partners walked away from the car.

The truck driver shook his head in agreement. "You ain't got to worry about me, son. I ain't about to give you no problems."

Buddy smiled and sat back. It looked as if his part of the job would end up being a snap. The man he had to watch didn't appear as if he would give him any trouble. His eyes surveying the street, he wondered again if his father would show up. He had lied to the other men about his father's whereabouts. He was well aware of Eldorado's habit of showing up at his numbers house during this time of the day.

4

THE TELEPHONE IN Eldorado's car rang sharply.
He reached over and picked up the snow white receiver. The phone in his car was not a luxury. Anything
that contributed to his work as much as the telephone
did was a necessary tool. Every day, as each number
came out, he was informed by telephone. If he happened to be in his car, he would still know what the
number was before it hit the street.

"Hello, Bob, long time no see. I should say that's
a good sign. The less I see and hear from my lawyer
means everything is running smoothly." Eldorado let
out a brief laugh, then said, "Okay, break the sad news
to me. I know you ain't calling me about my love

life."

For the next two minutes he listened quietly, then he spoke softly into the receiver. "Okay, Bob, you did the right thing. You say the bondsmen are on the case, so by the time I get downtown you should have the girls out, right? That's cool, then; where should I meet you, in the bondsman's office or at your house?"

He waited until the cold metallic voice answered him, then he hung up the receiver. Eldorado changed his direction. He had to come up off the northbound freeway and catch the freeway going south. Instead of heading for his numbers house, he was now on his way to his bondsman's office. When he arrived downtown, the women were already sitting in the bondsman's office. They both stood up as he entered.

Shirley rushed up and embraced Eldorado Red. He held her arms and slowly pushed her back off of him. "Okay, Momma, just take it easy now while you pull my coat to what the deal is."

For a minute she tried to look him in the eyes, then glanced away. "I don't even know how to explain it, Red. We did some dumb shit, and this is what we get for our stupidity."

Red's lawyer, Bob Ellis, stood up from the chair in front of the large, dark brown desk that filled the small office space. "Hey, Red, let's get this paperwork settled. I'm due back at my office."

Red nodded easily, as if he and the lawyer had just finished a dinner date. "Oh, yeah," he began, "it can't be but one thing that kept you here this long, Bob. You must want some money."

The lawyer chuckled loudly. "That's the thing I like about you, Red, you don't beat around the bush. If you have something to say, you come right out with it."

The tall, redheaded bondsman grinned at the two men. Gene Elliot walked around his desk and shook Red's hand. "You read him right, Red; money is the only thing that could possibly hold our friend anywhere for over ten minutes."

Shirley walked back to her seat and sat down beside Dolores. The men ignored the women as they laughed and talked back and forth. It wasn't too often that their business brought them together. And yet, they had been friends for over ten years.

"Well," Red stated, "how much is the damage? I thought I was good and paid up, Bob, but I guess you have other ideas on the matter."

Bob smiled encouragingly. "You were ahead at one time, Red, but that tax case of yours has eaten up all the money you had paid in advance, so I decided I'd wait to bring it up today." He glanced around and then asked quietly, "Unless you'd rather wait until you can come into the office where we can have some privacy."

Before either man could answer, Gene spoke up. "If privacy is what you want, you guys can use my back office," pointing toward the back of the small building.

The bondsman's office was one fairly large room divided into two parts by some cheap paneling. The rear office was a part of the main office, also partitioned with paneling. In effect, the one large office had been made into three smaller offices.

"No, no, that's not necessary," Bob stated quickly. He removed a notebook and wrote down a figure. "This is just about what you owe," he said, holding the note under Red's nose.

Without replying, Eldorado removed his bankroll and peeled off three one-hundred dollar bills. "Now that should bring us up to date, shouldn't it?" he asked quietly.

Using the chuckle that had become part of his style, Bob took the money and stuffed it into his pants pocket. "Yes, yes, by all means. That makes us just about even-steven, Red. Yes, that covers everything but Gene's money, but I'll leave that up to you two gentlemen." Bob reached out and shook hands with both of the men, then headed for the door. "As I was saying, I have to get back to my office. Very important client coming in. So, if you guys can handle the rest of it without me, I'll take my leave." Bob Ellis wheeled on his heel and started towards the door.

Both men waited until the lawyer had left before getting down to business. "Now," Red began, "that takes care of him, Gene, so the only thing left is straightenin' out my account with you."

With a shake of his head, the bondsman confessed, "No, you don't owe me anything yet, Red. You're well paid up in advance." To prove his words, Gene walked back to his desk and removed a piece of paper with some figures written on it. He held it out to Red.

Eldorado Red shook his head, refusing to take the

paper. "Naw, man, that's all right. You ain't got to prove a damn thing to me. I'm just glad to hear that I'm paid up."

Gene folded up the slip of paper. "Well, anyway, Red, you're two hundred in front. If you want to fatten it up, it's up to you. You generally stay ahead five hundred, but the two hundred is good enough. I'll get your people no matter what it costs—within reason, that is."

"Let's hope it never has to come to that, Gene," Red stated as he held out his hand. "I'll be gettin' on back to my business then, since everything has been taken care of down here."

Smiling encouragingly, Gene reached for the outstretched hand. "It's always wonderful to do business with a man like you, Red. I'm sorry you haven't got the time to have a drink with me," Gene stated, then added, "It's a shame that the only time we can get together nowadays is when someone has had the bad luck to get busted, but that's the way it is. Maybe you'll find the time to stop down and have lunch with me sometime. Just give me a ring and let me know in advance so I can set my schedule up. That's all you have to do."

"Okay, Gene, I'll tell you what. The next time I'm downtown, I'll stop by and you and I can slip out and have a drink, if nothing else. How about that?"

Gene walked Red to the door. "The ladies are due in court next week," he reminded him. "If you should come down with them, I'll have a taste over here at the office to wake you up after getting up that early."

Both men laughed as the women joined them. "You just do that," Shirley said, cutting in on their conversation. "I know I'll be dry as a bone after sitting in that damn courtroom all day."

For just a brief second a frown appeared on Red's forehead, but it was gone before anyone but Dolores noticed it. He glanced away from Shirley, not wanting her to know that she had made him angry by cutting into their conversation. That was one of the reasons he had broken off their relationship many years ago. She had the habit of always jumping in where she wasn't supposed to be. She wanted to be more important than she really was.

"Of course, Shirley, you know you're welcome," Gene stated as he held the door open for them. "Until next week, then," he said and patted Red on the back as the man went out.

Everybody was silent until they got in the car. Shirley made it a point to get in the front. When Dolores started to climb in with her, Shirley spoke up. "No, honey, don't sit there. I want to talk to Red as we drive home, and I can't very well carry on a conversation from the backseat."

Dolores studied her icily. She started to mention the fact that Shirley could talk just as well from the back of the car as from the front. But since she had just recently started working for Red, she didn't want to appear fresh. She knew that the older woman had aroused his anger. She slipped across the car seat and climbed in the back, glancing up at Red. She saw the anger in his eyes and decided that she had done the right thing.

Red watched as the women changed positions. His jaw tightened, but he didn't interfere. He'd have rather had the attractive young girl sitting next to him, but business always came first. He could always drop Shirley off and decided at once that that was what he would do. He would get rid of her old ass as soon as possible.

Red waited until he had pulled out into the fast flowing traffic before speaking. "Well, let's hear how your foolishness brought all this shit down on you."

"Not my foolishness," Shirley stated quickly. "Our foolishness."

"Well, whichever, let's hear it!" he ordered sharply. The woman's attempt at evasion was getting on his nerves. But then again, whenever he was around Shirley she managed to get on his nerves.

Shirley started talking slowly in a low voice that grew louder as she recalled the events of the day. Eldorado Red listened in silence. He couldn't imagine how someone would allow a few damn roaches to run them out of their minds. Both women running out into the streets with the policy slips in their hands, out of their goddamn minds because of a couple of roaches!

Exasperation was in his voice as he asked sarcastically, "Just what made these roaches so horrible? It ain't the first time either one of you have seen roaches, so why get so upset?"

"You'd have to see it yourself to believe it!" Dolores said, speaking up for the first time.

Red didn't want his anger to show so he remained quiet until he had it under control. "I guess you had the foresight to give Auntie Dee enough money to catch a cab home?" he asked sharply.

"Now, honey," Shirley began, "you know I'm not a fool. This isn't something I do every day. It's never happened before in all the years we have worked together, so I should get the benefit of the doubt. Of course I sent her home in a cab. As soon as Gene got her out on bond, I gave her the money to get home. In fact," she added, "I sent Dolores outside to wave a cab down for her. As strange as she looks, she might not never have got one to stop."

Which way should I go from here, he wondered coldly as he drove along. It was inconceivable to him that his pickup women had done something that stupid. For a minute he debated going by the house and seeing this terrifying collection of roaches himself. Maybe then he could understand the women's story, because as things stood, he couldn't bring himself to believe that what they had seen could be that shocking.

"What you should do," Shirley said, seeming to read his thoughts, "is to go there and witness it yourself. Then, and only then, will you be able to understand what we are talking about."

Impatiently he made a right turn. It was the only way, he reasoned. If he didn't follow it up, he'd never be able to put any trust in the women. Driving like a madman, it took Red only minutes to drive the large Cadillac back to Auntie Dee's house. When he got there, both women refused to go into the house with him.

Red had to laugh as he got out of the car. The women were really frightened. Red made his way up the walk. He knocked loudly on the door, then stepped back as Auntie Dee opened the door for him.

"Hi, sugar," Red yelled in greeting as he barged into the house. "I see the police didn't shake my baby up too much."

The older woman followed him into the house, shaking her head. "It never would have happened," she screamed in his ear, "if it wasn't for them silly women you sent by here."

He agreed with her, then walked straight back and parted the curtains that separated the front room from the kitchen. Red took one step into the kitchen and stopped. He backed up quickly. He could feel his nerves jumping. He shook his head in disbelief. "Goddamn, woman, what the fuck are you doing? Raising roaches?"

She laughed coldly. "It ain't no use fightin' um. As quick as we kill them, more come back. They don't really bother nobody, so we don't bother them."

It was too much! He couldn't believe his eyes.

"I'll send you somebody that will get rid of them goddamn roaches, Auntie. You can bet on it." With that, he staggered out of the house. There was no need for the women to ask him what had happened because they already knew.

As he started up the motor, he shook his head in wonder. "It's unbelievable," he murmured softly as he drove away from the curb. "I owe both of you an apology. I can well understand how it would affect a woman, 'cause it affected the shit out of me."

"What should we do?" Shirley asked. "I'm all for cuttin' them loose anyway. The pickup ain't worth stopping for really, and now this." She shrugged her shoulders.

"Naw," Red said quickly. "I promised their brother I'd do what I could for them, so after a good exterminator goes through that house, there won't be a roach problem, you can bet on that."

The women fell silent after that. Eldorado Red picked his way back across town driving now much slower than before.

5

TUBBY LED THE WAY up the stairs towards the apartment. Samson and Danny followed closely on his heels. When they reached the apartment, Danny removed his pistol and placed it under the two dinners he carried.

For a brief second, Danny hesitated before knocking on the door. This is it, baby, he told himself, his mind racing. It's too goddamn late to back out of it now. He could feel the back of his leg trembling and hoped that the other two men hadn't noticed. He gained strength from the knowledge that Tubby was on one side of the door with Samson on the other.

It seemed like an eternity before Danny got around

to lifting his arm and knocking. The sound seemed to carry up and down the long hallway. The men glanced up and down nervously, hoping nobody would look out of one of the other apartments.

Each man felt fear in one way or another. Samson feared the repercussions that he knew would come. The people inside the apartment they were going to rob meant nothing. But what he did fear was the anger of Eldorado Red.

Slowly the door opened, then stopped as the chain inside the apartment reached its limit. A man peeped out.

Danny held up the dinners so that the man could see. The eye examined the thin, short black man at the door. "Where's the rest of the dinners, man?" the man asked sharply.

"Right there on the floor," Danny replied, pointing where the man couldn't see. It was a gamble, but it paid off. The sound of the chain coming off could be heard, then the door slowly began to open.

Samson didn't wait for the door to open completely. He jumped beside Danny and kicked as hard as possible. The door flew open and Samson leaped into the room with his gun drawn. The doorman cursed, clutching at his bleeding nose. Danny and Tubby were right behind Samson. The ski mask Tubby had put on covered his face completely.

The men and women inside the room were frozen at their adding machines and typewriters. Nobody moved; everybody stood or sat as if they were suspended in an airless vacuum. The sudden arrival of the three men with guns had frightened them witless.

Samson motioned with his gun at a closed bedroom. Danny rushed over and kicked the door open. He stuck his head in, "Nobody," he yelled back as he retraced his steps.

Again Samson beckoned with his gun, this time it was to the bathroom. Tubby checked it out. The men moved around the room with the experience of men who had worked on robberies before. No move was made unless it was necessary. All the time the men checked out the apartment, Samson kept the rest of the people under the sight of his gun.

Finally, Samson beckoned towards the table that held the money. He had had a hard time keeping his eyes off the stacks of money. The greenbacks were the prettiest sight he had ever seen. As Tubby made his way to the table, removing a large burlap bag from his belt, Samson removed some tape from his pocket and tossed it towards Danny.

"Tie the two men first," he ordered sharply, never taking his eyes completely off the men. He noticed the shotgun propped up against the wall and grinned. Speed had paid off. The man responsible for protecting the women had been caught napping. He was at least ten feet away from the shotgun.

As soon as Tubby had all the money, he brought the bag over and dropped it at Samson's feet. "Help the short man out tying the folks up," Samson ordered as he removed another roll of tape and tossed it to Tubby.

The loud sound of the telephone ringing froze the

men in their tracks. Samson beckoned with the gun.
"Finish it up," he yelled, his voice showing strain. He
watched impatiently as the men went about the slow
business of taping up the women. The hands had to
be taped in the back of each person, then their mouths.
After that, the men taped their feet.

"That's all right, don't worry about the feet,"
Samson directed sharply as another phone began to
ring. The sound of the two phones ringing began to
get on his nerves.

"If one of you gals don't want a bullet in your
fuckin' head, you better stop that goddamn whis-
perin', 'cause it ain't goin' gain you nothing but trouble," Samson yelled, as the women began to gain
some control. Their initial fear was wearing off, and
now their minds were busy trying to figure out a way
to stop the men from leaving with the money.

Samson knew instantly what was wrong. They were
taking too much time. You couldn't take forever on a
robbery. It gave the holdup victims time to think.
Another phone began to ring. Somebody really wanted to know what was going on at the apartment.
Samson tried to rush his men.

"Fuck the gags, just get those last two bitches tied
so we can make our move," he ordered. He grabbed
up the money bag and moved toward the door. "It
don't make no difference if they scream. If the police
show up, they'll play hell trying to explain all these
fuckin' adding machines."

Finally Tubby finished tying up one of the women
and he walked toward the door. "Get that fuckin' mask

off before we step into the hallway," Samson ordered. Though he never raised his voice, there was that quality of leadership about him that he would not stand for a mess.

As soon as Danny had joined them, Tubby turned around so that the people inside the room could see only his back and removed his mask. He opened the door and stepped out into the hallway, Samson and Danny followed him closely.

The hallway was empty. But as soon as the men closed the door of the apartment, one of the women let out a scream. It was loud and threatening to the holdup men, but Samson stopped them from panicking.

"Hold still now," he ordered sharply, "don't run. Fuck that bitch screaming, it don't have nothing to do with us." He led the men down the stairway. "Let the bitch yell her head off. By the time somebody answers, we should be on our way."

When they reached the street, Samson made sure his men didn't walk too fast. He had to fight down his own desire to break and run for the car, but somehow he managed to find the necessary control. His appearance to the other men was one of coolness and control and that helped to relax them.

Samson walked around to the driver's side of the car. He opened the door and held it open. "Listen, bud," he said to the prisoner, "we don't want to hurt you, so I'm going to explain to you one time what I want you to do. If you should do something different, I'm going to bust a cap in your black ass, is that clear?"

The catering truck driver shook his head in agreement. "Okay then, now we ain't took your money or
nothing, so you ain't got no problem, right? Now,
when you get out, I want you to walk straight across
the street and keep walking right on between them
houses over there, without looking back. Is that
clear?"

The man nodded his head. "Okay then," Samson
stated, "let's get going. Don't forget, don't try and
look back so that you can get a license number,
because if you do, I'll have to shoot you." He never
raised his voice, but again there was that controlled
tone in it that said that here was a man who meant
exactly what he said.

As the catering truck driver got out, Samson slid
behind the wheel and started up the motor. He pulled
away from the curb slowly, all the time keeping his
eyes on the man walking toward the houses. The man
never looked back as he walked swiftly between the
structures. Samson grinned and pressed down on the
gas pedal.

"How did it go?" Buddy asked excitedly as he
pulled the duffel bag over into his lap and looked into
it. "Goddamn," he cursed with glee, "I don't know
how much we got here but it sure looks like we done
ripped off a winner."

"Pass me the goddamn wine," Tubby ordered as he
began to relax. It was over. They had got away with
it. What had started as a possible daydream for them
had finally become a reality.

"You know what," Buddy exclaimed loudly, "I think I'll take my share and go buy me a Cadillac." In the sudden silence that followed his words, he continued. "Yeah, that will really show up the old man. I asked the bastard to buy me one, and he wouldn't do it. Now, I'll just pop up with my own." He laughed coldly, not bothering to pay any attention to the men around him.

"You will my ass!" Samson stated harshly. "What the fuck do you think this is, some kind of game? We didn't risk our freedom and lives so that you could have something to throw in your father's face."

The other men remained silent. It was Samson's play; he was the leader and he would handle it. Buddy glanced at him in surprise. "What you talkin' about, man? You don't believe you're supposed to tell me how I'm to spend my share of the money, do you? I mean, I went along with you giving orders, even though I'm the one that set this thing up. I'm drawing a line somewhere, man."

As he spoke, Samson didn't attempt to disguise the contempt in his voice. "Listen, punk, I ain't goin' say this but one time. Ain't goin' be no motherfuckin' Cadillac bought by nobody in this crowd, and I mean it. If you buy one, you better sleep in the motherfucker, 'cause we goin' set the motherfucker on fire with you in it if we have to. Now, I ain't goin' let you put us on front street with your old man, kid, and I mean it. So the best thing you can do is pay attention and do like I ask. I ain't trying to run your life or nothin' like that; I'm just trying to put protection on us."

'Shit!" The word exploded from Buddy's mouth. "I don't see how my buying a Cadillac would put you guys on front street no kind of way. What I eat don't make you shit." He sounded like a spoiled kid who had had something taken from him that he shouldn't have had in the first place.

"Listen, my man," Samson began, "let me try and pull your coat so you can see where I'm comin' from. If you popped up with a Caddie for a ride, your old man's got to get to wonderin' where you got the cash, so the next thing he'll do is have his watchdogs check out your friends. That's us. Now the rest of these guys are going to be spendin' their money on clothes and things like that, so when the watchdogs come around, it's goin' ring a bell with them. How come these guys got sharp all at once, plus you with the heavy ride, adds up to us knockin' off the joint. Even a blind man can dig where I'm comin' from, Buddy." From the expression on Buddy's face, Samson felt certain that his words hadn't meant anything to the younger man. He stared hard at the younger man, scowling. His heavy eyebrows came together and seemed to bristle as his facial features appeared to become stony. His lower lip protruded and his hands shook as he fought to control his growing anger.

"Take it easy, baby," Danny said easily as he noticed his friend's temper beginning to get the best of him. From years of associating with the mild-mannered Samson, Danny knew the symptoms. Whenever Samson's face seemed to turn into a hard mask of

brick, it was time for somebody to give him plenty of
room.

"Hey, man, watch that light!" Tubby yelled as they
almost ran through a red light.

"Goddamn it!" Danny cursed sharply, "there's a
fuckin' police car sittin' on the side of that gas sta-
tion. It's a good thing you stopped in time."

As Samson backed the car up out of the intersection his mind cleared. When the light changed he
pulled off slowly. As they passed, the policemen gave
them the once over closely.

The rest of the trip was finished in silence. Samson
pulled into Tubby's mother's driveway. He drove all
the way into the rear of the driveway, stopping in front
of the garage. The garage behind the ranch-style brick
house had been converted by the men into their hangout. They had put couches, chairs and a record player inside, making it a decent place where they could
relax, play records and dance whenever they brought
any girls over.

Buddy pulled the duffel bag out of the car. Tubby
glanced up at the house as he took his key out and
opened up the garage. The men filed in in single file.
Danny pulled the door closed behind him and locked
it. The men gathered around the dinner table that was
actually used for gambling. Samson grabbed the bag
and turned it upside down, spilling the money out onto
the table.

"Motherfucker!" Tubby exclaimed loudly, "just
look at the motherfuckin' greenbacks. Goddamn, I
ain't never seen that much cash in my life. Look at

it. You mean to tell me that motherfuckin' Eldorado
Red picks up this much cash every day? Sonofabitch,
it's unbelievable, man, I just can't believe that one
dude can handle that much cash."

"Well, you better start believing it, boy. This was
just one of the nigger's joints that we knocked off.
He's got at least three more joints just like the one we
knocked off, ain't that right, Buddy?"

Buddy nodded his head in agreement. He was too
shocked by the sight of the money to speak. It was
one thing to talk about the cash, but quite another to
have it in front of you and realize that it was really
yours. Buddy had expected seven or eight thousand
dollars on the job, but from a glance, it seemed that
it was much more. Had Buddy been staying at his
father's house for the past week, he would have
known that it was much more. Eldorado Red had
closed up one of his number spots and combined it
with the one the men had knocked off. So instead of
knocking off the take of one joint, they had ripped off
the money from two places.

Samson began to count out the money slowly so
that there would be no mistake. When he reached ten
thousand dollars, he sat back and grinned. "Boy oh
boy, it looks like we done hit the big one after all."

He glanced at the men sitting around the table; their
faces were lit up as if the Messiah had just come down
and given each man his most desired wish. The men
had foolish grins on their faces. Samson smiled at
them and then finished counting out the money.

"Well, boys, looks like we got something like four

thousand dollars apiece. It comes to just a little over sixteen thousand dollars," Samson stated softly.

"Yeah, baby, that's sweet, but how about Red's other joint that we were supposed to knock off? Just because we got hold of a little bread, are we supposed to forget our plans?" Buddy stared around at the men trying to find out if his words penetrated.

The other men glanced away from his inquiring stare. The only man who could meet his glance was Samson. "It ain't what you're thinking, Buddy. First of all, didn't nobody have any idea that we would rip off that much money on the first job. We ain't even split the cash, yet here you are asking about when we goin' take off the other house."

"Bullshit!" Buddy exclaimed loudly. "I know what it is. These guys are shortstoppers, that's all. A little bit of bread is going to their heads. Okay, so we got four grand apiece, so what? How fuckin' long do you think four grand will last? It ain't nothin' but chump change for a player, but for a poot-butt, it's big cash." He didn't bother to disguise the contempt in his voice. "Yeah, that's the whole fuckin' thing in a nutshell. Here we got a chance to go for the whole hog and you guys want to accept the asshole!"

Samson pushed the piles of money over to the men. "Yeah, Buddy, what you say makes a lot of motherfuckin' sense, but I can still understand why these guys hesitate. This is the first time either one of them has ever had this much cash for their own, so quite naturally they want to enjoy spending it."

"Yeah, Samson," Buddy replied, "I can dig that too,

and it's really the first time I've ever had four grand at one time, even though I'm ashamed to admit it. Yet there's a damn good chance for us to more than double this little bit of bread. Ain't no sense in foolin' yourself 'cause all it is is just a little amount of cash."

The idea of doubling the amount of money on the table appealed to all of them. "What you got in mind, Buddy? You mentioned this other joint, but you ain't never really pulled our coat to it, like you did on this one," Danny stated as he pulled his roll of money over and began to push it down into his pocket. His mind was really on just one thing: he wanted to blow. Once he got his fix, he didn't care what they did.

Now that he could see that he really had their attention, Buddy started talking seriously. "It's like this, man. Red's got this joint over on the east side where he's been trying to build up his night numbers business. Now, if we go in there and hit it tonight, they wouldn't expect us. But…." He had to raise his hand for silence as the men let out a yell. "Just a minute, hear me out first," Buddy yelled, screaming the men down. "If we hit the joint tonight, they won't expect it, but if we fuck around and wait, Red's goin' get his mind right and put up some protection. I mean, it goes without saying, anybody can see it."

Tubby shook his head back and forth; it was too much for him and he knew it. "Man, I want to enjoy the money we got. If something goes wrong, we blow everything."

"Can't nothing go wrong. I know the place like the back of my hand. I used to work there so I know just what I'm talking about. If we move before they change their procedure, it will go off easier than the job we ripped off this afternoon." Buddy picked up his money and slammed it down on the table. "Goddamn, man, I'm trying to give you guys a birdnest on the ground and you're trembling like a hound dog shittin' birdseeds."

"Let me give it some thought," Danny said as he walked over and picked up the phone. "After I get my blow I'll be able to think a hell of a lot better," he said apologetically.

"Well, I'll be a motherfucker," Buddy screamed. "Here I'm trying to get you guys to take off a caper that will put big stuff in our raise, and this guy is worried about buying some dope." He turned on Samson who had remained silent. "You see what I've been telling you, man, about a dope fiend. That's all the motherfucker has got on his mind is drugs."

"Keep your voice down," Tubby ordered sharply. "Ain't no sense in lettin' everybody in the neighborhood know our business."

"What the fuck is that motherfucker talking about anyway?" Danny said sharply, holding the phone in his hand. But then he got his call and began to talk into the receiver. "Hey, Reno, this is Danny. I'm over to Tubb's joint, in the back, man. Yeah, you know where it's at. It's the same place you brought that coke last week. Dig, my man, how about dropping off two spoons of boy and a hundred dollar bag of girl." He waited silently, then asked, "Yeah, my man, how long will it take? I want it as soon as possible." He nodded his head, then replied, "Okay, just blow your horn like you did last time. I'll come out to the car." He hung up the phone and glared around at Buddy. "Now that's finished, let's get down to the real deal. I didn't sit out in the car today when that job went off like somebody I know. Plus the fact that that same nigger is planning on sitting on his ass out of the way, safe, whenever this other job goes down, so don't give me that dope fiend shit. I don't want no labels put on me by a motherfucker who ain't takin' no chances and still getting his complete share of the take."

Tubby laughed harshly. It did his soul good to hear somebody put Buddy in his place. He had always feared the tall, slim, cold-eyed man, so he never checked him the way Danny had. Tubby actually feared physical violence. He was well read, and he believed that Buddy was really a psychopathic personality. The man's childlike hatred of his father revealed to him an emotional immaturity that led to impulsive acts, which frightened Tubby.

"Okay, okay," Buddy said and tossed his hands in the air. "What do you guys want me to do, go in the house with you so that every motherfucker in there will recognize me? Is that what you want? 'Cause I don't give a fuck. I'll go in with you motherfuckers if it will make the job easier."

Finally Samson interrupted. "Hey, Danny, I heard you order all that coke, baby. What you goin' do, set it out for your partners?" His words broke the tension in the garage, as he hoped they would.

"You know me, Sammy, whatever I have belongs

to the rest of you as long as I ain't sick."

"If you would have said something, Danny, I'd have gave you another hundred on some girl, man," Tubby stated. "Shit! I like coke as much as the next man, so if you want to, you can call him back and get another hundred-dollar bag.

"Naw, Tubbs, not right now. I just got enough coke to make us feel good before going on this job, if we decide to take it off," Danny answered. "Too much girl and we'll be too froze to take care of our business, you dig where I'm comin' from?"

The sound of a horn blowing in the driveway set Danny in motion. He damn near ran out of the garage. The slim, light-complexioned man sitting behind the steering wheel of the powder-blue Cadillac grinned as Danny hurried toward the car.

"Hey, Reno baby, I'm glad to see it didn't take you long to get here," Danny said as he climbed in the passenger side of the car.

"It don't never take me long when a guy spends a yard and a half like you're doing," Reno stated. "You ain't short, are you, Danny? 'Cause if you are, man, I can't do nothing about it. The coke don't belong to me, man, so I got to have the right amount."

For a brief minute Danny stared at the small man. You lying motherfucker, he said to himself as he stared Reno down. The man had hit his pride, so when Danny removed his money, he pulled out the whole bankroll and flashed it under Reno's nose.

Danny got the reaction he had hoped for. "Goddamn, Danny, what you rip off, man, a bank?"

Reno asked as he stared at the huge roll. He let out a whistle and watched closely as Danny removed two hundred-dollar bills.

"You got change for a hundred, ain't you, Reno?" Danny asked as he dropped the bills in Reno's lap.

"Naw, my man," Reno said pushing back one of the hundreds. "You got change yourself, Danny. As big as that roll is, ain't no way in the world for it to be only hundred-dollar bills."

All at once Danny experienced a warning chill. An alarm went off in the back of his mind and he realized he had made a mistake. "Naw, man," he said with a grin, "we went out to the track this afternoon and I caught the twin double for two grand."

"Oh, baby, that's sweet," Reno replied, knowing the man was lying because he had been out to the track himself that day and he knew the twin had only paid six hundred and some change. Why was the man lying? he wondered idly as he pulled out his small bankroll. Reno had taken a beating out at the track, blowing part of his bag money, and that was the main reason Reno had said he couldn't stand any shortage.

Quickly Danny put the hundred-dollar bill back and tried to remove a fifty without Reno getting a good look at the size of his bankroll. He cursed inwardly as he ran through the money trying to find a fifty. Everything on top was a hundred and he had to part ten of them before he found what he was looking for.

Reno counted the hundred-dollar bills under his breath as he watched Danny. He realized that it must be over two grand in that roll. He believed he counted at least nine or ten one-hundred-dollar bills.

As Danny held out the fifty, Reno spoke softly. "If you should want to make a large buy, Danny, I can fix you up with some bad raw dope. You can put a five on it and it will stand up. I mean," he continued, trying to make a quick sale for big money, "you can make that roll grow to at least four times its growth. And that ain't no bullshit, Danny, I'll stand behind my dope."

"Okay, baby," Danny answered quickly, "don't go to running your mouth about this roll I got, and I'll spend a nice piece of cash with you no later than tomorrow."

"Don't worry about it. I'm like the blind man," Reno stated as Danny got out of the car. "I'll be waitin' for your call."

As Reno backed out of the driveway, Danny watched him go. After this rip tonight, he decided, he'd buy a nice amount of stuff and catch the first thing smokin' out of town. Yeah, that's just what I'll do, he told himself as he headed back toward the garage.

6

THE PHONE CALL CAME just as Eldorado Red was dropping Shirley off at her apartment. He waited until she had gotten out of the car before picking up the receiver.

As Dolores was climbing into the front seat, she heard Red curse. She knew instantly that something was wrong because Eldorado Red didn't make a habit of swearing. As he asked questions into the receiver, his voice took on a chilling, deadly tone. She could feel goose pimples rising on her flesh. Whatever it was, Dolores decided, she was glad it didn't involve her. She realized at once that he was in a killing mood. She had never seen a man in a killing mood before, but something inside of her told her that this man was.

"Okay, I'm on my way. Don't let anybody leave until I get there," Red said into the phone. "Naw, don't even think about calling no police. What the fuck's wrong with you, can't you think? Okay then, you know we don't want no cops in on this. We'll handle it ourselves." Slowly, Eldorado Red hung up the receiver. "Can you drive, Dolores?" he asked quietly.

Dolores stared open-mouthed at Red. For a minute she couldn't answer him as she wondered how the man had gained control of himself so fast. She had been frightened by his outburst, even to the point of wondering if he would take out some of his anger on her.

"Well?" he inquired rather harshly, bringing her back to reality. "Can you drive or not? I've got to make a move."

"Yes, yes, of course I can drive," Dolores said.

As the young woman jumped out of the car and ran around to the driver's side, Red lifted up the armrest and slid over to the passenger side. Now he could do what he needed to do without waiting. As the woman got in behind the steering wheel, Red lifted up the receiver and began to place his calls.

"Hello, Copper-head, is that you?" Eldorado asked as the car pulled away from the curb smoothly.

"Uh, Red," Dolores began, hesitating briefly, then continuing as Red put his hand over the telephone receiver and looked directly at her, "you didn't tell me where I'm supposed to be going."

He laughed briefly, and with that laugh the sting of

his words were gone. "Goddamn it, girl, you're right. I got so much on my fuckin' mind I forgot to give you directions, didn't I? Drive over to the pad where you turn in your figures every day, Dolores." With that, Red turned his back to her and picked up the conversation. "Hey, Copper-head, this is Eldorado Red, man. I need you and your crime partner." He glanced at his wristwatch. "How long will it be before both of you can get over to my house?"

"Damn, baby," the voice on the other end exclaimed shrilly, "Tank took off this morning for Florida. Everything seemed quiet so he decided to go visit his mother. She's gettin' up in age, you know."

"Damn!" The word exploded like a time bomb. "I didn't even know the nigger had a mother!"

"Well," Copper-head answered, his tone changing slightly, replacing the jocular mood he had used at first. Now there was a deadly edge to it, causing Red to realize that he had said the wrong thing. "That's something all of us have, Red, no matter how much of a wrongdoer he is. Even you got one, my man."

"I'm sorry about that, Copper-head, I didn't mean it like it sounded. My old lady is dead, and I figured Tank being our age, his parents had passed away too."

Copper-head realized at once that that was as close as Red would ever come to an apology. Besides, he knew the man hadn't meant any harm in the first place. "Don't worry about it, baby, let's get down to the nitty-gritty. Why can't I handle it by myself?"

"That's dead, Copper-head. Somebody knocked off my main house. I want you and Tank on the case.

There were at least three or four people in on the job, the way I see it." Red hesitated, then continued, "How are the chances of you gettin' in touch with Tank and having him catch the first thing smokin' back in this direction?"

"Goddamn good!" Copper-head replied, drawing out the words. "If I can get him on the phone, he should be back here sometime in the morning."

"Fine, you take care of that, Copper-head, and don't forget, money ain't no problem. Whatever it takes, I'll spend it." For the first time since getting his call through, Eldorado Red remembered the girl driving the car. "Listen, Copper-head, I can't really talk right now because I'm in my car. But I'll tell you what, you meet me over to my crib in about an hour. No, give me an hour and a half. I'm running over to the joint and rap with the people who were there."

For a minute Red just held the receiver and listened. "Yeah, that might be better," he replied quickly. "Why don't you catch a cab; that way, we can use my short for whatever runs we'll have to do. You can stay out to my pad, too, until we get some kind of light on this shit."

Eldorado Red searched his pockets until he found a cigarette. "Here's the address to the fuckin' place. You got a pencil so there won't be a mistake?" Quickly Red gave him the address over the phone and then hung up.

Dolores glanced over at him as he lit up his smoke. "Somebody robbed our house?" she asked simply.

With a quick nod of his head, Red answered her

without speaking. She realized that he was too busy
with his thoughts to hold a conversation with her. For
the rest of the ride, they were silent.

When they reached the apartment building Red led
the way up the steps, running most of the way. Dolores
had trouble keeping pace because of her high-heeled
shoes, and when they reached the upper floor Red was
way ahead of her. By the time the door opened,
Dolores had managed to catch up.

"Hi, Benny," Red said to one doorman as he pushed
past. "Where the hell were you when these guys came
barging in?" he asked sharply, turning on his other
doorman whose job it was to handle the shotgun.

Alvin Blue wiped the sweat from his brow before
he replied. "They took us by surprise, Red. It happened so sudden that I didn't know what was happenin' until they had barged past Benny."

It didn't slip past Red that Alvin was trying to pass
the buck. "Yeah, well, let's hear it. I do want to know
how the fuck three gunmen got through that goddamn
door! That's what the fuck you guys been gettin' paid
for all these motherfuckin' years. Not for your looks,
but to see that this kind of shit didn't jump off."
Eldorado's voice was cold as ice; the people listening
realized that somebody's job was going to be blown.

"They used a guy dressed in a catering service outfit," Benny said quickly. "I mean, we been orderin'
food for years, Red, and nothin' like this has ever happened." Now Benny was sweating. This wasn't the
laughing, joking Eldorado Red he was used to talking to. Before him was a man who seemed to be made

out of stone, and all of the people in the room could sense it.

Alvin believed that Red was just mad at Benny. His nerves settled down as he decided to make his role in it as small as possible. "Yeah, Red, I saw Benny go to the door and I waited until he gave me the okay sign, then I started helpin' out the gals. You know the way I do, whenever they get busy. I try and help out whoever seems to be in the hole."

"I don't want no bullshit, Alvin," Red said harshly, turning on the tall, gray-haired Negro, "so don't try and con me, man. I don't feel in the mood for that shit. Both of you were wrong, you both get paid to make sure this kind of shit don't happen. Them broads are paid to run the fuckin' machines, not you, so don't give me no shit about helpin' one of them out. That ain't what you're paid for, so it ain't no kind of excuse!"

The women moved around nervously. The tension was high inside the small apartment. Dolores moved back against the wall, trying to make herself as inconspicuous as possible, and the rest of the women followed suit.

The sound of a sharp knock caused everybody in the apartment except Red to jump. "Who could that be?" one of the women asked suddenly, then realized she had spoken and tried to disappear behind the woman next to her on the couch.

Benny glanced at Red nervously. "Should I answer it?" he asked timidly.

Eldorado Red stomped over and jerked the door

open. "You made damn good time," Red stated as the tall, husky black man entered.

Copper-head glanced around at the gathering of people. "Looks like you're herding a bunch of frightened cows to pasture," he stated coldly, his mouth opened in what was supposed to have passed for a smile, but instead revealed a mouthful of rotten teeth.

For the first time since entering the apartment, Red felt like he could relax. If the people in the room knew anything, Copper-head would get it out of them. He glanced around at the women. One of them finally gathered her nerves together enough to ask, "How long are we supposed to stay here, man? We've been here since this morning."

It became quiet enough in the apartment to hear a roach crawl. Copper-head fixed the woman with his icy stare. "You're impatient, huh?" he asked softly. "Here this man has lost thousands of dollars yet you don't have the time to try and help him get a line on who may have taken his money, is that right?"

The heavyset black woman gathered her courage and continued. "It's not that I don't want to help, it's that there is nothing I can tell him that would help him. I don't know anything about those young men that came in here."

"Why don't you let us be the judge of that, Mrs...."

"The name is Jones, Mrs. Jones, young man," she replied to Copper-head rather harshly, her tone demonstrating how annoyed she was becoming.

"Let's take them in the bedroom one at a time, Red," Copper-head said as he looked to Eldorado Red for approval. "Maybe that way we can get a line on what really happened here."

Red agreed and led the way towards the bedroom, but he was stopped by Mrs. Jones' sharp voice. "What the hell is going on here? We don't have to stand still for nobody's interrogation. I don't see any police badge on anyone."

"You seem to be the only one in the room that's really trying to hide something, Mrs. Jones," Copper-head stated. When he had spoken to her before he had been polite, but now his voice was flat and cold. "This way, please," he ordered. "Since you're in such a hurry, we'll give you the privilege of being the prime suspect in our case." Copper-head held the bedroom door open. Eldorado Red went in and sat on the bed.

Mrs. Jones didn't budge from her spot. "Suppose I'm not interested in that privilege and decide that I've wasted enough time here already today and go home, then what?"

"In that case," Copper-head stated, not bothering to look at Red, "I'd think you'd be tired of your job here and didn't want it any more." Before she could reply, he continued, "Plus the fact that I'd have to think that you must have a nest egg of cash hid away or a large cut of the take from this robbery."

For them to think that she could really be involved in the robbery was beyond her imagination, but it had suddenly dawned on her that they were taking the thought seriously. The hard, cold-faced young man in front of her was not smiling; he was dead serious about it. If she refused to talk to them, they would really believe that she was involved in the robbery.

"Of course I'll talk to you," she said slowly, stuttering as she walked past Copper-head into the bedroom. "Mr. Eldorado, I don't mean to cause any difficulty, but you see, I have a baby-sitter at home with my two daughters and I know she'll be mad because I've kept her over her regular time."

Red stood up and removed ten dollars from his pocket and gave it to the woman. "Here, maybe this will make her a little bit less angry," he pushed the money into her hand.

For the next two hours the two men talked to each person in the apartment until there was no one left but Dolores. "What about the young broad out there? I see you left her for last. You want me to call her in now?" Copper-head asked. Lines of fatigue were showing in his face that hadn't been there earlier. The toil of trying to read minds was telling on him.

"Naw, that ain't necessary," Eldorado Red answered quickly. "I know where she's been all day, even though that wouldn't have stopped her from settin' it up if she had wanted to."

Both men fell silent, each deep in his own thoughts. Finally Red asked, "What about Tank? Did you manage to get in touch with him?"

"Yeah, everything's cool on that side of it. He said he'd catch the first thing flying out tonight. I'm supposed to pick him up at the airport at three o'clock in the morning," Copper-head stated dryly before changing the subject. "I don't think we got anything to go on from them folks we just talked to."

"I seem to have got the same feelin' while we was talking to them. It wasn't leading anywhere, but we can't give up. I want them niggers, bad," Red stated coldly.

Copper-head took out his cigarettes and lit one. "I somehow feel that you're overlookin' something, Red. Don't try to think about it now. What I want you to do when we get to your house is fix a nice drink, relax, then sit down and write out a list of everybody, I mean *everybody*, who knows about this house."

"Maybe you're right, Copper-head. Right now I'm trying to think too hard. Maybe after I relax I'll be able to think better," Red answered quietly.

"I'll tell you what let's do," Red said as he got up. "Let's get the hell out of here and run over to my place. We can relax better and maybe, just maybe, I'll get a line on what happened. Somebody might call or something. A thing like this, Copper-head, can't stay quiet. People hear about it, talk too much, and maybe somebody might want to do me a favor and pull my coat. You never know about things like this. Something will jump off, I'm damn sure of that."

It was dark outside when they reached the street. Red glanced up and down, then turned to Dolores. "Honey, you feel like going over to my place and acting like the woman of the house tonight? I might just need a good hostage."

"I don't mind," she answered quietly, afraid to say no. As they piled into the car, something was about to jump off, but it was altogether different than what Eldorado Red had in mind.

7

AS EVENING SHADOWS began to fall, Buddy glanced out of the window of the garage. He released the torn, polka-dot curtain and let it fall back in place. He turned and surveyed the other occupants in the room openly and coldly. The contempt that he so openly displayed was lost on the other men as they continued to snort up the rest of the drugs. Buddy hated drugs—coke, heroin, pills—it didn't matter, he hated them all. Ever since his younger sister had died from an overdose when he was seventeen, he had taken a strong dislike to narcotics.

"How long, how long, man?" he inquired to no one in particular.

"Just be cool, baby," Samson replied lightly as he took another snort of the small pile of girl in front of him. "Danny, you about finished, baby boy?" he asked as he snorted up the last of the dope he had on his cigarette pack.

For the past hour, Buddy had been trying not to look over in Danny's direction. He couldn't stand the sight of the blood running down the man's arm, as Danny methodically sought the elusive vein.

"It ain't but a minute now, partner," Danny stated as he slowly pushed the bulb and the heroin flowed into his vein. Buddy watched the man as he jacked the outfit off, allowing the blood to run back into the dropper. Frowning in anger, Buddy looked away.

If I ever have reason to take off another play like this, he promised himself, I'll surely use somebody other than those motherfuckers. "Well, Danny," Buddy began, "if you're finished, we can get the fuck on with our job before it's too late."

Danny squirted the water out of his outfit onto the floor as he cleaned out his works. "I'm ready whenever the rest of you guys are," he stated loudly, getting up and stretching. "Damn, but that's some good blow."

Samson stood up too. "Come on Tubbs. Let's go get rich."

The heavyset man hesitated for a minute. How he wished that he had enough nerve to tell them that he wasn't going. The last thing Tubb wanted was to go on another stickup. He had prayed that the first one would go off without a hitch, promising his God that if he got away clean, he'd never go on another stick-up again as long as he lived. Now, here he was, four or five hours later, getting ready to go on another robbery. Tubby sighed deeply and stood up; the cocaine had made his nerves worse than ever. He was actually trembling as he followed the men out of the garage.

"I wish we had somebody in the crowd tall enough to pass for a damn policeman in uniform," Samson stated as the men got in the car. "It would go off sweet as a motherfucker then."

"What's wrong, man," Tubb inquired in a frightened voice, "you don't think nothing is going to happen, do you?"

"Hell, naw!" Buddy replied for Samson, "he's just talking, that's all. It would be nice if somebody had on a policeman's outfit, but since we ain't got it, we have to operate with what we got."

Tubby let out a deep moan. "I don't like it. If we get greedy, like we're doing, we're just asking for some kind of trouble. You guys are nuts, really. Here you go and take off a joint for over fifteen thousand dollars and you guys still ain't happy. How many small-time operators like us ever get the chance to really knock off fifteen grand and get away with it?" He looked at the others before he continued. "Have you guys stopped and asked yourselves that? Naw, I know you ain't, 'cause if you had you'd be back at the garage tossing money in the air."

"Bullshit!" Buddy stated, making the word sound like dirt. "When you refer to small-time punks, you're only talking about yourself, Tubby. Everybody else in this ride considers himself a big boy, not a small-time operator." Before Tubby could answer, Buddy continued. "The only difference between a small-time stickup man and a big-time operator is the size of the job he takes off, Tubby. From the size of our job, we ain't small time. Just the fact that we have over fifteen grand put up shows we ain't some nickel and dime motherfuckers out here trying to get fix money."

"Run it down, baby," Danny yelled as he came out of a nod. Spit ran out of the corners of his mouth as he fell back into another nod.

"Goddamn, Samson, look at that motherfucker! You think he's goin' be able to take care of his end of it?" Buddy asked, nodding his head in Danny's direction.

Samson glanced in his car mirror. "Don't let it worry you, Buddy. I'm the one who has to depend on Danny backin' us up, not you. You ain't got no problem sittin' out in the ride except the seat might become hard on your ass."

"Tender buns," Danny yelled out, then began to laugh wildly. "You didn't tell why our partner has tender buns, Samson, baby. You been holding out on me or somethin'?" He continued to laugh wildly, disregarding Buddy's angry stare.

"You better watch yourself, Danny. I don't play that shit, man," Buddy stated coldly.

"No kiddin'," Danny replied. "You don't cook but you eat, baby boy." There was no laughter in Danny's voice now. He seemed to be cold sober.

Now it was Samson's turn to laugh. "You see,

Buddy, he ain't noddin' no more, is he?"

Buddy didn't bother to answer but instead turned around in his seat and ignored the rest of the men.

"I sometimes wonder, man, how the fuck did we ever allow this cat to start fuckin' around with us. He comes on funny most of the time, just like some white kid trying to be hip. If the rest of the guys in Chicago are like you, Detroit can do without them cats."

"Naw, it ain't like that," Tubby said, speaking for the first time since getting in the car. "I got some cousins over there, man; ain't no kind of shit they take from nobody. Them brothers is real swingers. They belong to some kind of rangers or some such club. All of them brothers stick together, too. It ain't like the Big D where so many brothers is startin' to snitch on each other."

"They tell me the guy who's always talkin' about other people snitchin' is the one you have to worry about the most," Buddy said, trying to cut somebody else up since Danny had done such a good job on him.

Instantly Tubby went on the defensive. "You ain't got no cause to call me no snitch, Buddy. Ain't no mud on my name and ain't none ever been on my name, ain't that right, Samson?"

A slight frown crossed Samson's face, then disappeared just as quickly. If there was one thing Samson hated, it was for someone to make a yes-man out of him. He realized, though, that Tubby was weak and needed someone to boost up his ego. Right now, since they were going on a job, he needed Tubby in complete control of himself.

"That don't even need to be answered. If you
wasn't cool, Tubbs, you think me and Danny would
be fuckin' with you? Especially on a big job like this,
baby. Don't nothin' but big fellows fuck with big fellows. Your problem is, Tubby, you don't realize just
how mellow you are." Samson slowed down and made
a right turn, then added, "After we rip off this job,
baby, you goin' have to fight the young bitches off."

Buddy didn't bother to look out the window to conceal the scorn in his face. Why, he wondered, did
Samson bother to fatten up the frightened little fat
man? Everybody knew he was scared to death; a blind
man could see that. Buddy laughed as he wondered
if the fat man ever pissed on himself while taking off
a job. How the fuck they ever talked him into getting
up the nerve to try sticking up someone was beyond
Buddy's imagination. It was true enough the guy
looked the part. He was big and ugly, but that was as
far as it went. His heart wasn't even as big as a pump-
kin seed.

"Make a left on the next corner, Samson," Buddy
directed. "Now, don't forget," Buddy began, "this
ain't like the last one. This is a private house, a two-
family job, but don't nobody stay upstairs." He waited until he was sure everybody had his ears open, then
he continued. "Now, I came over early this morning
when there wasn't nobody here and cleaned up the
joint. When I took the trash out, I went in the basement and opened the window in the rear, one that
nobody would notice unless they were lookin' for it.
That's why I want you to be sure to lock it as soon

as you enter. That way, when they start trying to figure out how you guys got in, they won't have no way of knowing it was through the rear basement window."

"When we get through this window," Danny said, taking a serious interest in what was being said, "we ain't goin' run into much trouble upstairs, right?"

"Shouldn't be no problem for you guys," Buddy replied coldly, still angry with Danny for shooting up before taking off the job. "It ain't but three old men upstairs. Every one of them is damn near fifty years old. The only gun in the joint is a shotgun, and it's always in the bedroom out of the way. Now, if you guys creep up the steps right, you'll take them completely by surprise. I mean it, they won't know what hit them. More than likely, they'll be too busy figuring up the night's take to even hear you guys coming up."

"It sounds sweet," Samson said. "If it hadn't, I wouldn't be out here tonight, not after that first job. The first one was so mellow that I can't help but to take Buddy's word on this second one. The guy is giving us information that some guys would give their left nut for."

"Right there," Buddy said, "that's right, pull in the alley. We goin' park behind the vacant house next door. Then I'll get out and lead you guys to the window so there won't be no mistake. I put a little grease on the motherfucker so it would open and close without any kind of noise."

"My man, you do know how to take care of business," Samson stated, smiling broadly. He followed the directions and parked. The men got out quietly and made their way through the alley.

"Goddamn it!" Danny cursed loudly, kicking a bottle away. They all glanced at him but no one spoke.

When they reached the gate, Buddy lifted the latch and led the way into the yard. Now the men walked on their tiptoes. Buddy stopped at a window in the rear of the house. He slowly raised the old window frame. It came up without a sound.

Samson was the first one through the window. He climbed in slowly, followed closely by Danny. Samson felt his way around, making sure there was nothing in the way of the other men. He helped Danny down, then both men waited and helped the heavyset man through. Tubby had trouble, and for a minute, the men thought that he was going to become stuck in the window. Tubby got his head and shoulders in, but that was as far as he could go. Buddy pushed from the outside while the men in the basement grabbed his arms and pulled. He groaned as they pushed and shoved until finally they managed to get the fat man through.

"Goddamn it," Danny said under his breath so that his voice wouldn't carry. "That's the last time I'll ever take a chance like that. We could have blown the whole thing while fuckin' with his fat ass!"

Tubby was hunched over rubbing his stomach. "What you want to do," he said as he straightened up, "stay down here and cry over something that's all over, or get on with it?"

The enveloping blackness of the basement was so

complete that the men couldn't see each other. As Samson led the way, they had to hold each others' hands. Samson lit matches as he slowly made his way across the basement floor. When he reached the stairway, he attempted to empty his mind before climbing the wooden steps. He could feel his blood racing; there was a heightened sense of awareness about him.

When Samson reached the top of the stairway, there was a closed door in front of him. He prayed quietly that it wouldn't be locked. As he leaned against it, he could hear the hum of an adding machine.

"You guys ready?" he asked calmly, not able to see his men in the darkness. Samson removed his pistol, then made sure each man had his gun out also. It was an unnecessary stall, but for some reason, he wanted to delay the final act. Finally he couldn't put it off any longer; he could feel the men growing restless behind him. He tried the knob and the door opened.

Samson looked at his own men as he stepped into the light of the kitchen. Each of them had put on ski masks. He remembered suddenly that he also had a mask. He quickly pulled it out of his pocket and slipped it on.

Sounds of activity were coming from the front room. Samson took a deep breath and burst through the open doorway that led to the dining room and eventually to the front room. As the men moved quickly through the dining room, they passed a bedroom door. Without stopping, Samson beckoned to Danny with his gun.

Danny jerked his head up and down acknowledg-

ing the silent order. He stopped and pushed open the
bedroom door. To his surprise there was a couple
inside busy making love. His silent entrance took them
by surprise. The woman was the first one to notice
the man standing in the doorway holding a gun.

Without warning the woman screamed. The scream
brought Danny back to reality. He had been admiring
the young golden body reclining on the bed in a
lover's embrace. She was tall and slim, and her long,
lithe body was even more beautiful than Danny had
imagined a woman's could be. Since he was strung
out, sex was something he rarely thought about, but
the unexpected sight aroused him completely.

The sound of the woman's scream brought the two
men working in the living room to attention, but it
was too late. They found themselves staring into the
barrels of the two pistols held by the stickup men.

Tubby glanced over his shoulder. The scream had
almost scared the shit out of him. He still didn't know
what had happened. Danny hadn't come out of the
bedroom yet. From where Tubby stood, he couldn't
see him standing in the doorway.

"Go check it out, the scream and everything,"
Samson ordered sharply. "I can handle these two."

One of the middle-aged men in the living room
began to inch his way nearer the shotgun lying on the
table. "Go ahead, reach for it!" Samson told the man.
"Let's see how big a hole this .38 can make in your
damn ass."

The man jerked his hand back as if he had touched
something hot. "Just be cool with that gun, blood!"

the man said as he stepped farther away from the shot-gun. "We ain't goin' give you guys no trouble, so don't hurt nobody."

Samson moved over to the table and picked up the shotgun. The silence that enveloped the room was like a blanket. The men being held up stared at the shot-gun as if it were a deadly snake. There was fear in their eyes as they stood motionless, waiting to see which way the gunmen were going to go. People had been killed in numbers robberies and each man hoped that it wouldn't happen in this one.

"What's holding you guys up back there?" Samson asked, yelling so that the men in the bedroom could hear him.

Tubby reappeared from the rear. "Danny's waitin'," he said, not being quick enough to stop himself from mentioning Danny's name. "He's waitin' on this broad to put some clothes on. They were back there fuckin' when he barged in on them," Tubby smiled under his mask, then added, "Boy, that's one fine bitch back there."

"We got more important things on our mind than some fuckin' bitch," Samson warned. "Hey, you, what's your name?" Samson asked the man who had tried to reach the shotgun.

"Mike, everybody calls me Mike," the man stated shortly, acting as if it pained him to speak.

"Uh huh," Samson began, smacking his lips. "I'm goin' ask you one time, Mike," he said, pulling back the hammer on the double-barreled shotgun, "where the fuck is the money?"

Mike swallowed, then glanced over to his partner. He nodded his head at a brown bag sitting on the floor next to the table.

"Damn," Samson cursed. "If it had been a snake it would have bit me," he said, realizing he should have spotted it himself. He broke the gun open and took out the two shotgun shells. Then he walked over and looked down at the bag. It was full of money and white envelopes. The loose money was all in small bills.

The sound of a woman's shrill voice came to them as Samson set the bag down on the couch. "You don't have to point that thing in my direction," the woman said as she walked out of the bedroom and came into the front room. She was followed closely by a slim, brown-skinned man attired only in a pair of shorts.

Danny brought up the rear, holding his gun on the couple. The woman was the one who caught Samson's eye. It had been a long time since he'd seen a woman with such a beautiful color.

"Goddamn," Samson said sharply, "what the fuck are you doing here with these old bastards?" He was unable to explain to himself why he felt the woman to be out of place in that house.

"Turning tricks, goddamn it," she answered abruptly. "Is anything wrong with that?" Samson admired her magnificent teeth as she spoke.

"Naw, baby, I guess we all have to live," Samson replied as he let his eyes roam all over her. She had put on her skirt, but Danny hadn't allowed her time to put on anything but that and a bra. Her breasts stood out in the tight-fitting bra like ripe melons.

"You trick with all these guys?" Tubby asked, not able to hide the emotion in his voice.

She turned on him like a cat. "I don't see why that should be any of your business," she yelled. Though she was scared, she had the feeling that the men in the masks wouldn't hurt her. Why would they have gone to the trouble of hiding their faces, she reasoned, if they were going to kill everybody in the house? Ever since she had started coming over and tricking with the men in the numbers house, she'd feared something like this would happen. The men handled too much money, and she had never believed them to be strong enough to stop someone from robbing them. Now as she stared at the men with their hands up in the air, she remembered the idle boasts they had made about what they would do if someone tried to knock them off. Every word they had said had been bullshit. She could see the fear in their eyes. They were actually more frightened than she was. The thought gave her strength and she smiled.

"You find something funny?" Samson asked. "Or were you thinking how much fun it would be if we all decided to lay a little dick in you before we left?"

His words wiped the smile off her face. Her eyes became hard and she suddenly became frightened. It was the masks—but she didn't realize that that was the root of her fear. They made the men seem like beings from another world, and she couldn't relate to them.

Tubby wet his lips and scratched at his nuts. "Man,"

he began, slobbering slightly, "you think we might have time to knock off a piece of that? Goddamn, I ain't never laid no broad like her." The fat man was trembling as he stared at her.

It was tempting, but Samson decided not to take the risk. "Man, are you nuts? Fuck a piece of pussy—we come for the cash, that's all. You want to blow this thing for a piece of ass, man?"

The tall, slim girl leaned back against the wall with relief. For a minute she believed she would have to take all the men on—something that definitely didn't appeal to her. She tried to stop her legs from shaking, she didn't want the men to see just how upset she had become.

"Tie them up," Samson ordered, tossing the rolls of tape to his two henchmen. "Step on it; we want to get the fuck out of here as soon as possible."

Danny made quick work of his man, then moved on to the next one. Tubby had fucked around on his tying job so that Danny had to do it for him. Tubby moved towards the woman and made her sit on the floor and put her hands behind her back. As soon as he got her hands tied behind her, he began to touch her breasts. The more he felt the woman, the more aroused he became. He put his hands between her legs and played with her. She began to cry, and the more she cried, the more aroused Tubby seemed to become.

Samson had watched it all from the beginning. He had nodded towards Tubby when Danny had glanced at him. "Fuck that shit!" Danny stated coldly. "Fat-ass nigger, get your hands off that sister. I don't blame her for crying with your funky ass feelin' all over her. Get up, nigger, I say!" Danny raised his pistol and leveled it at Tubby. He couldn't explain it to himself but it made him mad to see Tubby pawing the woman.

Tubby scrambled to his feet. Without the pistol being pointed at him he might have chanced another feel. He had managed to get one finger up inside of her, but that hadn't been enough. To force three or four of his fingers up in her at one time would have been something, but the sight of that pistol pointing in his direction had completely wiped the thought from his mind. The only thing he wanted to do now was show Danny that he was doing as Danny asked. He knew the man was mad at him, even if he couldn't explain why.

"What's wrong, my man," Samson said as he gathered up the bag containing the money "don't tell me you got morals all at once?"

"It ain't that, brother, it's just that I don't like to see no sister debased or degraded like fat boy was doing her. She's a whore, yet his fuckin' behavior was so repulsive that it made her cry. Naw, man, I just can't sit still for no shit like that!"

"Well, fuck it," Samson said and shrugged his shoulders. "A little squeamishness don't take no man's masculinity away from him. I'll bet you'd like to lay her if I said we had the time."

For a second Danny struggled with his conscience, then he smiled under his mask. "You had me going for a minute," he said and laughed, "but I know you too well. You ain't about to lay around this joint while

we knock off a piece of ass, so let's get the fuck on
our way."

Both men laughed. As Samson started for the rear
of the house, he bent down and felt the woman's
breast. "You know, in a way, I can't blame the big
guy. This broad really has something to offer a man."
Samson got up from his knees and glanced back at
the victims. "Let's go!" he ordered.

The men made their way out of the back door,
Samson bringing up the rear. When they reached the
car they didn't see Buddy until he rose up from where
he had been lying on the backseat. As the men scrambled in, he asked excitedly, "How did it go? Was it
sweet, like I said?"

Nobody answered him until Samson got in and
started the motor. "Was it sweet?" Samson repeated.
"It was like taking candy from a baby. I mean it, it
was easier than the one we took off this afternoon."

The men laughed and joked as Samson drove out
of the alley. They could relax now; it was over. Buddy
opened the envelopes and took a quick count of the
money.

"I believe we got something like nine grand here,"
he stated and set the bag down. "It's kind of dark
inside the car, so I might not have counted right, but
I believe I'm close. Nine grand ain't bad."

"Nine grand ain't bad at all," Samson answered as
he sped away from the house they had just ripped off.

8

THE TWO MEN SAT around the living room in silence. The television was on but neither man seemed really interested in what was showing. Each man was deep in thought. In the kitchen, Dolores moved around, making the men something for a late-night meal.

"When you have something like waitin' on a plane to come in, the time moves slow as hell," Copper-head stated.

"Yeah, I know what you mean," Eldorado Red answered offhandedly. "Fuck, what the hell is that woman doing, growing the goddamn food?" Eldorado Red glanced at his watch. "Shit! It ain't twelve o'clock

yet! We still got over two fuckin' hours to wait for
that damn plane!"

"Man," Copper-head began, "why don't you take
that broad in the bedroom and give her some dick?
That way you'll kill some time and quit worrying me
to death about how slow it's passing." He had for-
gotten that he had been the one to comment on how
slow the time was passing.

Finally, after what seemed like hours, Dolores
appeared with steak sandwiches and iced tea. The men
grabbed up the delicious looking snack until there was
nothing left but the crumbs.

"Do you think it will cause you a problem to stay
overnight, Dolores?" Eldorado Red asked abruptly.

Damn! Dolores said under her breath. Here she had
been planning and scheming for the past month on
how to end up staying all night with this man, and
now here he was asking her. But there was no hint of
romance involved. It seemed more like he needed a
housekeeper than a lover. Well, if that's what he took
her for, she'd make damn sure she ended up being the
most expensive housekeeper he ever had.

"Yes, of course, Red. I'll stay and help you out,"
she replied quietly. She'd stay so long he'd have to
put her out, Dolores coldly reflected. This beautiful
house was the epitome of her dream, even if Red
wasn't the man she had daydreamed about sharing it
with. But all in all, the money he had would make up
for any shortcomings.

"Goddamn, Red, you use about as much finesse as
a bull in a glass building," Copper-head stated as he

grinned up at Dolores. "Now, if it was me inviting this fine young thing over, I'd have gotten up and took her into one of the bedrooms and talked a little shit to her. But you, you just come out with it. You want to stay all night, baby, just like that."

Dolores tried to blush, putting on an air of shyness. Eldorado Red just waved the matter down. He didn't really care if she stayed or not. The last thing on his mind was sex. If he wanted some pussy, he knew a hundred bitches to call.

The telephone rang sharply. The sound broke the silence that invaded the ranch-type home. Eldorado Red picked up the receiver. "Yeah!"

His facial features began to change as he listened. "What?" he exploded. "The hell you say! We're on the motherfuckin' way now. Don't nobody leave." It was an order. The way Red yelled into the receiver left little doubt to the people in the room that something serious had happened.

He slammed the receiver back down. "Let's ride, Copper-head. Them same motherfuckers have knocked off my other joint."

Copper-head leaped to his feet. "Looks like you got big trouble all right. We are just goin' have to show them that it don't really pay to fuck with your shit. It makes me and Tank look like poot-butts, too. Everybody in the know realizes that we're your enforcers. These punks just don't want to give us our proper."

For one of the few times in their relationship Red came down hard on Copper-head. "Maybe that's the reason they think my people done got soft. If it's true, I won't waste no fuckin' time replacing the soft ones with some young bloods who will take care of business. I want the fear of God put in these niggers, with no ifs, ands or buts about it."

As they rushed towards the car, Copper-head remained silent. There was nothing he could say. He was well aware that Red was upset. He'd settle down in time, but right now, the shock of it was riding him. Too many more blows like the ones he had received today and he'd be completely knocked out of the box. Nobody could stand it, not anyone Red's size anyway. It would take a much bigger numbers man than Red to be able to stand a fifteen- or twenty-thousand-dollar ripoff.

It was just lady luck smiling down on them that prevented them from getting a ticket on the way to the north end. Red broke every law in the books as he put his foot down on the accelerator and kept it there until they slowed down and parked. Copper-head let out a sigh of relief, thankful to be out of the car. High speeds always upset his stomach.

Red had been angry earlier, but now he was about to explode. His face had turned a dark red, and a vein in his forehead was so swollen that it looked deformed. He pounded on the front door of the house, forgetting that he had the key in his pocket.

"Why don't you slow down a little, Red? This is goin' take sharp thinkin'. Running off angry ain't goin' solve the problem. Just get control of yourself, then we can get to the bottom of this shit."

Eldorado Red glanced sharply at Copper-head. Before he could make an angry reply, the door opened.

Mike stood in the doorway. "Come on in, we been waiting for you," he said as he stepped aside so that the men could get past him.

Red stalked in, followed closely by Copper-head. Inside the living room were the other two men. They sat quietly, waiting for the questions to begin. Mike brought up the rear and quickly got out of the way and found himself a chair.

"Okay," Copper-head began, "which one of you would like to tell us what happened?"

Willie Brown, the man who had been in the bedroom with the woman, began to speak. "We were all sittin' in here gettin' the figures together when these guys popped up. They just came through the dining room as if somebody had let them in the back way." Willie held up his hand and added, "But that ain't possible because I had checked the back door when we came in. I always make sure it's closed and locked up tight."

As the man talked, Red lit up a cigarette and listened. "Wasn't anybody else here but you three guys, right?" he asked.

A funny kind of silence fell on the room, then Willie picked it up where he had left off. "Red, you know us. We been workin' for years with you. Don't nobody else work out of this house but us."

"Well then, just how in the fuck did three motherfuckers get in? Three guys just don't walk through the goddamn air without somebody hearing something, yet you guys want me to believe they didn't come in the back door. They didn't break no window to get in, they just popped up out of thin air, right?"

Exasperated, Willie tossed his hands in the air. "I can't understand it, Red, 'cause we didn't hear nothin' until it was too late. Then the motherfuckers were here."

"One was thin, the other fat, and the leader husky, right?" Copper-head asked.

"That's right! That's just how they looked. Plus, they called the thin one Danny." Before anyone could ask Mike any more questions, he added, "It wasn't no put-on either, Red. The fat guy made the mistake and then tried to catch himself, but it was too late." As Eldorado Red began to stare at him closely, Mike continued, "There's one more thing, too. I think the guy called Danny was an addict. He looked as if he had a long track on his hand. On the back of it."

"Good!" Red said. "That's a hell of a lot better than that shit we got from the other joint. You're sure of all this, Mike? You ain't just giving me a snow job now, are you?"

"No way, Red, no way in the world. And for what reason? I ain't got no reason to want to snow you. I want these punks caught, too," Mike reasoned quietly.

As Red continued to question them, Copper-head walked off. He examined the kitchen, then came back into the living room. "You guys touch anything back there?" he asked.

Willie Brown shook his head. The medium-sized

black man rubbed his protruding stomach as he tried to recall everything that might be important. "Naw, we made it a point not to bother anything back there since that has to be the way they came in."

A vague idea flashed through Copper-head's mind, but he couldn't put his finger on it. He removed a pad from his pocket and tore off three sheets of paper. "I want each one of you to write down every person that you know who's been in this house and who knows what goes on here." He passed out the sheets, then stopped in front of Red. "I'd appreciate it if you would do the same thing, Boss." He held out the paper. Red hesitated, then took it.

As the men got busy writing down the names, Copper-head went back to the kitchen. He examined all the windows, then went into the bedroom. He reappeared after a few minutes carrying an ashtray. "Who was the broad you guys had up here tonight, or was there more than one?" From the way the men jumped when he mentioned a woman having been there, Copper-head realized at once that he had hit on something.

The men tried to deny it, but Copper-head wouldn't accept it. "Stop lying!" he ordered sharply. "If you bastards ain't got nothing to hide about this robbery, don't let me keep catching you lying, 'cause then I'm goin' think you boys might have figured this robbery out all by your lonesomes." He removed a cigarette from the ashtray. The lipstick on it could be seen by everyone.

Eldorado Red's anger returned. "I don't want no

shit," he screamed. "If you motherfuckers had some whores up here, we want to know about it," he yelled, then turned on Mike. "How much fuckin' money was in tonight's take, anyway?"

"A little more than ten thousand dollars, Red. I don't know the actual figures. Willie and Jack was handling that."

For the first time the short, bumpy-faced man named Jack spoke up. "There was ten thousand, five hundred and sixty-two dollars in the night's take," Jack stated in a high, shrill voice. The sight of the cigarette with lipstick on it had frightened the man to death.

Reading the fear in the man's eyes, Eldorado Red pushed his questions home. "Now, Jack, if I find out you're lying to me, it's goin' cost you more than just this fuckin' job. You been workin' for me for over ten years now, so you'll kind of miss your paycheck, plus you're going to need some money for your hospital bill."

The mention of a hospital bill did the trick. "I ain't got no reason to lie, Red, honest. It wasn't none of my whore noway. I told Willie about bringing her in here in the first place," he said in his shrill, frightened voice.

"You lying little cocksucker," Willie yelled angrily. "You fucked the bitch as well as Mike, too. Every fuckin' one of us balled her, so ain't nobody excused." Willie turned to Red. "But she didn't have nothing to do with it, Red. She's been coming in here for over a year now, and nothing like this has happened."

Copper-head let out a grunt. "How about that! Can you speak for her pimp, too?" he asked sarcastically. "You guys put her name on them lists, plus any more whores you dumb motherfuckers have drug in off the streets. Red, it's a wonder your joint ain't been knocked off before now," Copper-head stated as he glanced over one of the men's shoulder to see what name he was writing. "You better put her address down there, Willie, and her phone number, so we can get in touch with her as soon as possible."

"I swear to you, Red, she ain't had nothing to do with this robbery, man. You should have seen the way them guys treated her. They wanted to rape her, right here in front of everybody. Especially the fat one, he couldn't keep his hands off of her. When he tied her up, he stuck his fuckin' hand all the way up her cunt, man. He caused the broad to start crying."

"Aw, bullshit, Willie, you goin' tell us a whore started crying because some motherfucker stuck his hand in her pussy? The bitch more than likely came all over his hand," Red stated harshly, then added, "I guess you guys know this just about knocks the wheels from under you as far as I'm concerned. All three of you knew I didn't want no bitches coming in this joint. Now you're the cause of me losing over ten grand."

"The girl ain't got nothing to do with it, Red," Mike managed to say. "Even if you fire me, it don't change matters. The girl didn't have anything to do with it."

Red glanced from one to the other. "This must be one hell of a whore, Copper-head, to have all these guys so sure she didn't set them up."

"I'd stake my life on it," Jack managed to say, before Red cut him off.

"You might have already staked it on just that, Jack."

Copper-head beckoned for Red to come back to the kitchen. "Suppose we stop by and pick up this bitch on our way out to the airport," he said, glancing down at his watch. "We got just about one hour left before we have to be there. So let's run over and pick up this bitch and take her along. When Tank gets off the plane, he can give me a hand gettin' rid of the bitch if it added up to being she's responsible for these stickups."

Red agreed, then added, "I don't really think she's responsible, Copper-head. Not because of what these old cum-freaks say, either."

"Why, then?" Copper-head asked.

For just a minute Red leaned against the window sill deep in thought. He turned around and faced Copper-head. "First, don't none of these guys know about my other joint, or if they know about it, they don't know where it's located, so I don't see how they could have set up both joints. Naw, it has to be deeper than what we've come up with so far. But still, we're not going to overlook this whore."

Copper-head led the way back into the front room. The small group of men fell silent at their return.

"Which one of you guys is going to show us where this broad stays?" Copper-head asked. "We ain't got no time for any bullshit, so let's get on with it."

Willie got up from the couch. He didn't like the idea of going by Vera's house, but he didn't have much choice. "You guys finish up here," Red said to the two other men before leaving, "and I'll talk to you sometime tonight when you come back to work." Red knew that he was going to have trouble trying to replace all three men at one time. If it had just been one, he could easily have handled that, but all three of them caused him a problem.

The men remained silent in the car as Red followed the directions Willie gave him. They stopped at an apartment building. "You think I better go up alone?" Willie asked nervously.

Eldorado and Copper-head got out without speaking. They followed Willie up the steps. The men took an elevator up to the third floor, where Willie knocked on the door.

"Who is it?" The sound of a woman's voice came floating out to them.

"It's me, Willie, honey." Willie blushed as the two men with him glanced coldly in his direction.

The door opened and Vera appeared, wearing a nightgown of black silk. The light from behind her made it possible for the men to see the outline of her beautiful body.

"I'll be damned," Copper-head managed to say as he stared at the beautiful woman.

Even Eldorado Red was taken aback by the loveliness of the woman. He stared at her like a country boy. As he looked into her eyes, he could feel his breath catching. It had been a long time since he'd

seen such a beauty. The woman standing before him
appeared to have stepped out of a dream.

"Well," she said coldly, "what the hell's the idea,
Willie, of bringing all these people up to my place?
You know I don't like strangers coming here."

"Then that makes us even, honey," Red stated
harshly, finding his voice. "I don't much like the idea
of strangers going to my place, either."

For the first time, Vera glanced up at the tall, light-
complexioned man. "If I remember correctly, I've
never been to your place," she replied rather sharply.

"I'm sorry about this, Vera," Willie began, "but you
see, it was this fellow's place that them guys knocked
off. I just happen to work for him. This is Eldorado
Red."

The name seemed to ring a bell with her. She
opened the door wider. "Won't you come in out of the
hallway?"

For a brief second the men hesitated, waiting to see
what Red would do. He led the way into the nicely
furnished apartment and took a seat on the luxurious
red couch.

"Now, how can I help you gentlemen?" Vera
inquired as she picked up a robe and slipped it around
her shoulders. It did little to hide what was underneath.

"We would like to know what you can tell us about
that robbery tonight," Copper-head asked harshly,
finally shaking off her spell. Now he could deal with
her as a person. At first, her beauty had completely
overwhelmed him.

"Nothing!" she stated coldly. "I don't know anything about it except that I was there when it happened and wish to God I hadn't been."

That really wasn't the kind of answer Copper-head had hoped for. "Then would you be kind enough, young lady, to tell us what your pimp's name is?" Copper-head took out the lists and began to look at them so that he would have something to do other than stare directly into the woman's eyes.

"I'm sorry, but I don't happen to have a pimp," Vera answered gravely. "And that's the truth, whether or not you believe me. I don't have a man."

Copper-head had pulled out the list Eldorado had made out earlier from the first holdup and the list that Mike had given him from the second robbery. One name from both lists jumped out at him. He opened his mouth to speak, then read the lists again to make sure. It was the only name that appeared on both lists.

"Red," Copper-head yelled, "who the fuck is this guy Buddy?" He turned the pages over, trying to keep his excitement down.

"Buddy!" Red exclaimed. "Buddy is my son, why?"

The letdown could be seen all over Copper-head's face. "Damn. Naw, Red, for just a minute I thought I had something. It seems your son is the only dude on the list who happened to know the whereabouts of both your joints."

"Well, he should," Red stated. "He has the job of cleaning both of them up every night."

Something was bothering Copper-head, but he

couldn't put his finger on it. "How about givin' me a key to both joints? Me and Tank will want to go over them," he said thoughtfully.

"Miss," Red said after acknowledging Copper-head's request, "would you be kind enough to ride out to the airport with us? I would like to talk to you a little more. Then we'll drop you back off."

Vera started to say no, but the man seemed so sincere that she couldn't turn him down. "If you'll wait a second, I'll slip into something," she replied. She disappeared into the bedroom and was back in minutes wearing a tight-fitting pants outfit.

On the way to the airport, Eldorado Red dropped Willie off and then caught the freeway towards the airport. They rode in complete silence.

Copper-head was absorbed in his own thoughts. Something was trying to come to light, but he couldn't put his finger on it. He knew that once he got in touch with Tank, between them they'd get a line on what was worrying him.

As Eldorado Red pulled into the airport and parked, Vera glanced over at the expensively dressed man. "I guess they hit you kind of hard, huh?"

He laughed coldly. "It's not just the small house they knocked off, but they knocked off my big house earlier in the day for close to twenty thousand dollars."

Vera managed a small whistle. "That's a lot of bread, no matter how you look at it," she stated.

"Yeah," Red said softly, "but it ain't goin' be worth a cent to them, honey, because you can bet your last dollar on it we're going to find out who those jokers are."

Copper-head got out of the car. "What you goin' do, lay out here in the parking lot or go on in with me?"

"You go ahead and meet the plane, Copper-head; I'll be sitting out here talking to the young lady. It don't take both of us to walk Tank back to the car," Red stated with a grin. He knew he was going to enjoy the fine company of the young woman next to him.

For some reason, Vera found herself drawn to the tall, light-complexioned man. He seemed so sure of himself. Maybe it was the fact that he represented big money. But money didn't mean that much to her. She made more than she could ever spend herself, so his money wasn't what drew her to him.

"You know, it's something about you, Red, that I really like. I believe that's the only reason I came out here tonight anyway, because you asked me," she stated, smiling up at him.

For the first time that day, Eldorado Red allowed himself to laugh. "Well, that's nice to hear. Coming from a woman with your looks, it makes me feel nice to know I'm thought about in that fashion."

They both laughed. It was spontaneous. In a matter of seconds, Vera found herself in his arms. They kissed slowly at first, then longer until they both could feel the tension running between them. The current was completed and the sparks flew.

The sound of someone knocking on the car window caused them to break apart. Copper-head got in the car and was followed by Tank.

Tank slid his suitcase in first, then maneuvered his huge frame into the backseat. "What's happenin', Red?" Tank said. "I thought you was havin' trouble. But I see you sure don't need our help. At least you shouldn't want it."

The men in the car laughed as Red started up the motor. They talked as Eldorado Red drove back to town. By the time they'd reached the city limits, Tank knew as much about the robberies as anyone else in the car.

For the first time, Vera had finally gotten some idea as to the scope of the robberies. She also realized just how big a man Eldorado Red was. There was nothing small about his numbers operation.

Red drove to his ranch house and parked in the driveway. Vera raised her eyebrows. "What's this? I just thought you wanted me to drive out to the airport with you, honey," she stated in a soft voice as she got out of the car and took Red's arm.

He led the way up to the porch. "I did, Vera, but that was before I found out how I felt about you. It may sound silly since I just met you, but that's the way it is. Now I don't want you out of my sight. I mean it. I've never met a woman before who I wanted to have beside me all the time, but they say there's a first time for everything." Eldorado made the statement quietly, and she could feel the sincerity in his words.

But words were not necessary because Vera felt the same thing. For the first time in quite a while, she had

met a man whom she really wanted to be with. To go
back to her lonely apartment now, without him, would
just cause her to have another sleepless night. A
woman living without a man to take care of was only
half a woman, and Vera knew it. It was why she felt
her life was so empty. But every man she met had
been interested in her earning potential and not in her.

Before Eldorado Red could put the key in the lock,
Dolores opened the door from the inside. The big
smile on her face died at the sight of the golden
woman on Red's arm. She managed to cover up some-
what, but Vera had seen it instantly. She wondered as
she stepped into the house if Dolores was Red's
woman. She decided she would find out as soon as
possible. If there was something she wouldn't stand
still for, it was sharing her man with another woman.
She believed she was too much woman for that. If a
man couldn't be satisfied with just her, then she didn't
need him.

Another person who noticed the exchange was
Copper-head. "Hey, honey," he said to Dolores as he
came in the door, "how about you fixin' you and me
a big drink. I think we both can use it."

At first Dolores started to tell him to get the goddamn drink himself, then she glanced at him closely
and understood that the man was just trying to be kind.
He understood more than she had realized. Then the
sight of the huge man coming in behind Copper-head
caught her attention. She didn't believe she had ever
seen such a width on a man. She stared at him in wonder; then it dawned on her that this man had been

brought in because of the robbery. Well, she was
thankful she didn't have anything to do with them.
Just the sight of him made her believe that the stickup men had trouble coming. The huge man's face was
as strange as the rest of him. It appeared to be made
out of rock. His eyebrows were shaggy and the dark
eyes that stared out were midnight black.

Unaware of the heartache he had caused, Red
stopped in the middle of the living room and intro-
duced the women. "Vera, this is Dolores; she's one of
my very best pickup girls." Before the women could
speak, he went on, not wanting Vera to get the wrong
impression. "Dolores was nice enough to stay at the
house tonight while I ran all over town trying to get
this shit straightened out." After introducing the
women, he again didn't notice Dolores grit her teeth
as she attempted to be nice to Vera, but it was a case
of hate on first sight. She realized instantly that Vera
was destroying her every dream. The big house was
disappearing faster than it had appeared in her life.
Before she could even put her feminine plans to work,
they were destroyed by another woman. From the way
Red looked at Vera, Dolores knew her scheming was
at an end.

Vera glanced around the house curiously. She could
well understand the other woman's anger. It wasn't
hard for her to see that Dolores had set her cap for
Red, but from what she could see, it looked as if he
hadn't even given her a tumble yet. If Vera had anything to do with it, she'd make sure he never found
the time. She had finally found a man that she really

liked and she had no intention of letting him escape.

Everybody made themselves comfortable in the living room and Dolores served drinks.

"We'll need to use your ride, Red," Copper-head stated, "until I can get across town and pick up my car. So if you don't feel like driving anymore, I'll take care of it."

Red nodded in agreement. "Ain't no kind of problem there, but I want you guys to stay here for the night. Get plenty of rest, then get on the case in the morning. Maybe you'll be able to think better after you've had a little rest."

Tank stretched his arms out. "That sounds good to me. We can get up and take us a quick swim in your pool back there, then get on the case."

"You like to swim, Vera?" Red asked, staring deeply into her eyes. She nodded that she did. "Good then," Red continued, "I didn't ask, but honey, I hope you don't mind staying here for the night. That way we can get up in the morning and have a good swim together."

"No, I don't mind staying tonight, as long as I stay with you," she replied, not bothering to lower her voice.

Her reply caused Red to grin from ear to ear like a schoolboy. "There is nothing in the world that would make me happier," he said as he stood up and reached down to help her to her feet. He led the way back to his king-sized bedroom.

If looks could kill, the look that Dolores gave them as they went past would have put them both in their graves.

Copper-head laughed and spoke to Dolores. "Well, honey, sometimes you can win some of them but not all of them, so if you don't mind taking second best, I'd be more than pleased if you'd join me in my room for a drink."

The hatred in Dolores' eyes made Copper-head step back. "That's all right, dear," he said quickly. "Just forget I offered it to you before you let your anger make you say something to me I couldn't overlook."

Dolores jerked her skirt up tightly, spun around on her heels and stomped out. "I think you better pull Red's coat tomorrow to get rid of her," Tank stated. "Don't make sense raising no snake in your house that's just lookin' for a chance to bite you."

Copper-head stared at the retreating woman's back. He removed the lists from his pocket and moved over on the couch next to Tank.

"Ya, Tank, you got a good point there 'cause it looks like Red might have a snake in his house that's already real close to him." Copper-head spread out the lists so that Tank could read the names that were on them. For the next hour the two men stayed in the living room talking and getting a closer line on what had happened earlier that day.

9

IT WAS PAST TEN o'clock in the morning before anyone appeared in the backyard at the pool. Everybody had ended up sleeping longer than they had planned.

Tank and Copper-head splashed water on each other as they enjoyed their early morning swim. They were both filled with the exhilaration of being alive.

"Man," Tank exclaimed loudly, "this is what I call living high on the hog." Using the palm of his hand, he splashed water in Copper-head's face. "Baby boy, you better enjoy it. It ain't often that you'll get a chance to wake up and step into your own fuckin' pool."

"You better believe it, Tank. Truer words have never been spoken."

The sound of the men playing around in his pool aroused Eldorado Red from a deep sleep. The first thing to meet his eye was a perfectly shaped breast. He blinked, closed his eyes, then reopened them. It all came to him in a flash. Slowly he opened his arms and that well-shaped bundle of joy slipped right into them.

"That's better," Vera whispered in his ear. "For a minute I thought you might like to go out and do a little participating with the other men. They sound like they're having so much fun."

"You must think I'm crazy, or do I just look sort of crazy to you? Which one is it, because a sound-minded man couldn't possibly think of leaving where I'm at right now." He pulled her tighter.

"Really now, Red. After what you put me through early this morning I'd think you'd have had enough lovemaking to hold you a lifetime." Vera's voice was husky and low as she whispered quietly to him. "Oh, honey, please, I don't think I can stand it if you're up to it. I'm really sore, you know?"

"Too sore?" he asked as he kissed each one of her breasts tenderly.

"Well, I don't know about that. I might not be too sore, but the only way I could find out would be by trying it," she giggled as she rolled over on her back.

Red slowly mounted the woman. "If it hurts you, Vera, just let me know," he said as he began to slowly force himself into her.

For the next twenty minutes they made love. The only sound coming from the bedroom was that of the large king-size bed. Every now and then a moan would be heard, but other than that, it was quiet.

The only person interested in what was going on in the bedroom was Dolores. She leaned against the wall outside the bedroom as she waited for her cab. A tear of frustration ran down her cheek as she stood frozen outside of the room. The anger she felt was all aimed at Vera. From her conversation with Copper-head she had learned that Eldorado Red had just met the woman the day before.

The sound of a car horn outside broke her out of her trance. She walked slowly from the house, aware in her heart that it would probably be the last time that she would ever be inside the house.

"I wonder who the fuck that is out there blowing," Tank said as he climbed out of the pool.

"More than likely it's the cab our girl Dolores called," Copper-head stated as he followed Tank out of the pool.

"Oh yeah, that jealous bitch. She ain't left yet?" Tank inquired as he began to dry himself off with a large towel.

"Naw, she hadn't when we came out, but she has by now. She was calling a cab then," Copper-head explained to his partner.

"Ummmm, oh well, that's the way the cookie crumbles at times," Tank said philosophically. "It's a good thing that broad pulled up, though, 'cause she spelled pure trouble for Red if she stayed around here." For a second he remained silent as he reflected on it, then he added, "From what I saw, Red acts as if the bitch didn't even exist. I mean, he completely ignores her, yet anyone with eyes can tell she must have been his woman or something, the way she digs him."

"Naw, that ain't it, Tank. The broad just brought that shit on herself. Ain't nothin' between them. From what Red said, he ain't never even balled her. He was going to when we got back from the airport, but that was before he met this Vera chick."

"How do you know all this shit?" Tank asked.

"I asked him!" Copper-head answered quickly. "I wanted to hit on this chick myself, so I asked Red yesterday if I would be steppin' on his toes if I tried to trim the broad, but he said he didn't give a shit. He was goin' try and trim the broad himself, like I said, but after one look at Vera, he must have completely forgot about it."

"After one look at Vera, quite a few guys would forget another bitch," Tank stated.

"Here, man, hit my back with this towel, Tank. I can't stand the feel of water on my back. Wipe it good 'cause I don't want it fuckin' up my silk shirt."

Tank did as he was asked. "What's on the program for today?" he inquired as the men started back toward the house.

Before replying Copper-head stopped on the patio and stared out at the neatly kept grass. "It's something I can't quite figure out, but I think the key to this whole motherfuckin' thing is back at the house they knocked off last night. I want to go find out how them punks got in, then we'll go from there."

"Yeah, it makes sense. It has to be a setup from where I sit. I can't see no other way around it, Copper-head. The guys just walked in. No way! Somebody had to pull their coat to what they were walkin' in on. If not, you couldn't pay them guys to walk in a num-bers house without knowing beforehand how many guns were there and who was furnishing the protec-tion."

"Uh huh, my mind comes up with the same fuckin' thought," Copper-head replied quickly. "Let's get the fuck on over there and check this shit out."

Both men dressed quickly. "I'll get the car keys, Tank, while you straighten up in here a little. Ain't no sense us leaving the bedrooms fucked up. I don't think Red has got a maid, so do what you can so it won't look too bad, okay?"

Tank nodded his head in agreement as he started to make up the bed. When he finished, he removed a pistol from under the pillow and stuck it in his shoul-der holster. Copper-head was waiting in the hallway.

"Well," Tank began, "it didn't take you long to get the car keys. Was the boss busy?"

Copper-head grinned. "I don't know. The cock-sucker wouldn't let me in the bedroom. He had left the keys on the dining room table."

"It figures!" Tank stated as they went out the door. "Just how much dough is the job paying us?"

"It's sweet, partner, you can bet on that. Whatever cash we find on the punks that took this off belongs to us, plus the fact that, if we ain't satisfied with it, all we got to do is ask for more."

"You mean everything?" Tank asked, surprised. "Hey, baby, the way I add that up, it's big stuff! Them punks ripped off over twenty-five grand, didn't they?"

"That's right, your adding ain't bad. Counting the take from both jobs, it's over twenty-five grand. That's why we have got to move fast. We don't want them punks to have no time to spend the bread. It don't take long to blow when you go to buying Cadillacs and diamond rings," Copper-head stated as he stopped to raise the garage door.

Tank let out a high-pitched laugh as they climbed in the car. "Yeah, I can dig where you're sure 'nuff coming from. If them punks have the time, all that cash will be blown." He waited until Copper-head backed the car out into the street before adding, "I think we had better bring this job to a close before the week is out."

"A week is too long!" Copper-head answered quickly. "If we can find something to go on at that house, we might just be able to blow the lid off this motherhubba before tomorrow night."

"As the hip white kids would say, groovy, baby," Tank yelled over to his partner, almost busting his eardrums in the tight space inside of the car.

After that, both men fell silent thinking about the job ahead of them. The fact that they would have to kill somebody didn't disturb them at all.

Copper-head pulled up and parked in front of the numbers house. The men sat for a moment staring at the building.

"Well, this is it," Tank said, opening his door. Copper-head got out and met him on the sidewalk. The men went up the walk side by side.

Suddenly Copper-head stopped and popped his fingers. "Those guys came in from the back, Tank, so let's walk around to the rear of the house. I've been inside, but I didn't have the time to examine the outside last night."

Without answering, Tank led the way around the side of the building. There was a dilapidated barn behind the house and where there had once been grass was now a dirt lot complete with rocks and bottles. The yard appeared to have been at one time the drinking bin of some aging wineheads. The large accumulation of wine bottles couldn't have come naturally.

Moving with the agile swiftness of a man much smaller than himself, Tank jumped up the steps and leaped over the broken one at the top. He landed lightly on the back porch. After a quick survey of the rear door, he jumped back down.

While Tank had been checking on the rear door, his partner had been kneeling down checking out the windows in the rear of the house. "They came out the back way," Tank stated as he joined his friend, "but from the tracks on the porch, they damn sure didn't go in that way."

"I got a hunch," Copper-head said as he got up out of the dirt, "that we'll find the answer to damn near everything we want back here."

Copper-head led the way, checking each window that he came to. Finally one of them opened easily

under his touch. He raised the window up. "It goes
up easy enough, that's for damn sure," he said as he
stuck his head inside the basement. He glanced around
in the darkness, then pulled his head back out. "We're
going to have to have a flashlight before we can check
out this basement right. It's completely dark down
there."

He stood up and knocked the dirt off his knees.
"Let's check out the trunk of the car for a damn flashlight, then we'll get on with it."

As they reached the car, Tank said, "You had better take a quick look in the glove compartment, too."

"Yeah, Tank," Copper-head replied, but there was
no bitterness in his words. "I'm glad you thought of
that. It would never have entered my mind," he stated as he took the keys out and opened up the Cadillac
glove compartment. The large silver flashlight almost
fell out onto the floor.

Both men laughed as Copper-head removed the
light. This time they went through the front door of
the house. Copper-head didn't stop, but led the way
straight back to the stairway leading down to the basement. As they went down the steps, Tank reached out
and hit the light switch. Instantly the whole basement
was flooded with light. The sudden light took Copper-
head by surprise. He stopped on the stairway and
stared around, then burst out laughing.

"Goddamn you, Tank, I see you're still thinking for
me. Why didn't you pull my coat outside that the light
switch worked?"

The two men laughed together, the way two friends

would do. Tank came on down the steps and joined his partner. Copper-head swung the useless flashlight back and forth as he led the way over to the half-open window.

"Hey," Tank yelled excitedly as he glanced at the window, "this motherfucker has got oil or something all over it!"

Copper-head grinned at his friend. "It's just about all out in the open now, brother. All we got to do is check and recheck. It's definitely an inside job, so it's just a matter of using a little common sense."

"Yeah, I can dig it. It's like a motion picture. It's slowly coming to the conclusion. I went over those lists last night thoroughly, and I saw something that's damn revealing."

Copper-head sighed deeply. "I think I know just what you're talking about. The same name keeps jumpin' off the motherfuckin' list yet it still don't make sense." Copper-head raised his hand, cutting off any reply. "I know what the goddamn problem is, too." He removed both lists from his pocket. His index finger stopped at one name in particular. "This has got to be our boy. He cleans up this joint, so who would have had a better chance than him to put the fix on the fuckin' window? Next, he's the only motherfucker whose name appears on both lists."

"In other words," Tank said easily, "this kid is the only one who really knows the whereabouts of both the goddamn houses."

"Uh huh. Next to Eldorado Red, Tank, he is the only one who knows, if we go by our list." Copper-head was silent for a second, then added, "I believe that Red realized this too but just doesn't want to face up to the fact that his own son has set him up."

"What happens if what we're guessing at now comes out to be the real deal?" Tank asked slowly as he lit up a Pall Mall.

Copper-head glanced over at his partner. "We already have the green light to make a hit, but I'd take the time to make a phone call or two."

10

VERA LAUGHED SOFTLY as she sat on the edge of the bed waiting for Eldorado Red to finish eating the steak dinner she had prepared. How long has it been, she wondered idly as she watched him finish up the salad, since she'd spent the day in bed with a man whom she really cared for? The time had gone by so fast. It didn't seem real. One glance out the window revealed that evening was quickly approaching.

"Darling," she began in a voice that sounded like chimes, "I can't really believe this day was real." She leaned over and wiped the edge of his mouth, then planted a kiss on his lips.

Red grinned up at the woman as he held the tray

of empty dishes out to her. "Well, you had better get
used to them, baby. After showing me that you can
cook like that, it doesn't leave me much choice. Either
you move in with me on your own, or I'll have to
kidnap you."

She laughed briefly. "I don't know, Red. Right now
you want me, but how about after we run into some
people or some close friends of yours ask you what
are you doing with that whore? Then what?"

He grabbed her arm firmly and turned her so that
she was facing him. "Let's be for real with each other,
Vera. I don't give a fuck what somebody might say,
and that shit about you havin' been a whore, I don't
care about that. Half the women who come here and
sleep with me are whores, and the other half should
have been whores, only they weren't turned out. No,
no," he said, and kissed her slowly, cutting off her
quick retort, "don't say anything, just listen. I want
you more than I've ever wanted any woman in my
life. It's not just for sex, either. I want you to be my
lady. I want you beside me when I go to sleep, and I
want you next to me when I awaken. Then when I get
up, I want you near me every minute of the day if it's
possible."

At the sound of his words, Vera experienced a sen-
sation of contentment that she had never felt before.
"Darling, I don't know what to say. I can't say no.
Only a fool would try and deny themselves something
that brought them so much happiness. Even if it
doesn't work out, I'll have today, tomorrow and
maybe the next one to remember. Yes, daddy, I'll

accept your offer and be your woman."

Now it was Red's turn to feel new sensations. He was overwhelmed with a desire to protect her, to hold her close, and to be tender to her. "You'll never forget or regret this decision, Vera," Red stated quietly as he pushed back the covers and started to get up.

Vera retrieved the food tray. "I'll take this back to the kitchen and straighten up back there while you take that shower you've been putting off all afternoon and, honey," she asked quickly, turning back toward the bed and blushing slightly, "is there anything I could get for you? Maybe run your bath water if you'd rather take a bath?"

"No, honey, if I let you, you'll spoil me so that I won't be able to do anything for myself."

They laughed and Eldorado smiled unconsciously as he opened his dresser drawer and removed fresh silk shorts. No matter how bleak some days could start off, he thought happily as he made his way to the shower, there was a ray of light. And in this case, he believed the impossible had happened.

Red stood outside the shower and adjusted the water until it felt suitable to his touch. The hot water running off his back helped to relax him. Once this stickup mess was over, he speculated, things would really change. He'd take Vera on a quick trip up to New York for a week or two, then Canada, and let her enjoy the sights of that beautiful country. The more he thought about it, the better he liked the idea.

As Vera moved around the kitchen cleaning up, she suddenly thought she heard some noise. She stopped

and listened closely. The sound of someone entering
the front door could be heard. Oh well, she reasoned,
whoever came in that way must have had a key
because she was sure the door had been locked. She
wondered idly if Dolores had decided to come back;
then the thought of the woman having a key filled her
with a cold rage. The intruder walked heavily towards
the kitchen. Only a man would walk that heavy, Vera's
agile mind quickly informed her. She let out a sigh of
relief. It was probably Tank or Copper-head coming
back to report. She frowned slightly at the thought of
the two gunmen. She was no fool. The fact that death
sat heavy on their shoulders didn't escape her. You
could almost smell it on them. And those eyes of
Copper-head's gave him away. Killer was written all
over him.

The sound of someone giving her the old wolf
whistle made her jerk her head around quickly. The
angry words on her lips died when she saw Buddy
leaning against the door jamb. He had one arm on his
hip and stared at her openly. His eyes seemed to
undress her as he let his glance go slowly over her
body. His open insolence was almost too much for
her.

"Well," he stated arrogantly, "looks like my old
man has a littl' more taste than what he generally dis-
plays."

From the look of contempt Vera tossed his way, the
average person would have paid heed, but Buddy
didn't care one way or the other. "Yeah, honey, when
the old man gets too pooped to take care of his busi-

ness some night, why don't you slip down the hall to my room and find out what a young man can do for you?" Buddy stated, then added, "That is, if you're going to stay around a while. Most of his women stay a week or two, maybe. You have to be exceptional to get that second week out of the old man, but," he allowed his eyes to run over her body again, "you look like you might just have what it takes to stimulate an old man."

Up to this point, Vera hadn't bothered to answer him. Now as she whirled on him with blazing eyes, the hot angry words on her lips died at seeing the naked arm reach out and grab him from the rear.

Buddy found himself jerked around by a stronger grip than he would have given his father credit for. The blazing eyes staring down at him were not the eyes that he was used to. The man staring wildly at him wasn't the same man he had grown to dislike. There was a murderous rage in his father and, for the first time in his life, Buddy felt fear.

Eldorado Red found himself too overcome with blinding rage to trust his voice. All he could do was shake the semi-helpless boy in his grip.

"Goddamn it, man," Buddy yelled as he found his nerve returning, "turn me loose. What's wrong with you, Red? You done lost your mind?"

Not bothering to answer, Red pushed into the kitchen and slammed Buddy back up against the wall. As he clutched Buddy by the collar, he found some control of his raging temper.

Vera watched from the sideline, afraid for the nasty

young man. Her anger was gone now and replaced by horror at what was happening. The last thing she wanted was to become the reason why a son and his father fell out. She reached out towards the struggling men weakly. Her gesture was completely ignored. Neither man really saw it.

"You dirty little sonofabitch, you," Red roared. "I've had other women come to me and tell me about some of the things you've said to them about me, Buddy, but I wouldn't believe them. No, I'd make up an excuse for you. They had to be wrong or lying. I've even went so far as to make one girl leave because she kept coming to me telling me the different things you'd said. Now I come to hear it with my own ears, yet I still don't want to accept it."

"Accept my ass!" Buddy roared, still trying to break the grip that Red had on his collar. "Take your whore-feelin' hands off me, man," he yelled as his anger began to grow.

Red brought up his left arm and slapped Buddy across the face. The sound was like an explosion. Before Buddy realized what was happening, Red slapped him again and then slammed him back up against the wall.

"Oh, my God," Vera cried out, "don't hurt him on my account. Please, Red, please don't. I'll leave, honey, you don't have to have this trouble over me. Please, please, just stop it."

The threat of her leaving did what nothing else could have. It brought Red to his senses at once. "If you leave because of this nigger, I'll kill him," he stated in a voice that left no doubt as to whether or not he was bluffing.

Slowly Eldorado Red released the trembling boy. "I want you out of my house, Buddy. Not tonight or later on, but now. Get your shit and get the fuck out of my life. I don't want to see you again, for any reason."

"That's damn cool with me!" Buddy replied as he attempted to straighten out his shirt. "You're true to form, Red," he stated coldly. "I don't expect anything else out of you. When you get finished using someone you kick them out. Ain't that the way you did my mother? When you was poor she was good enough for you, but as soon as you got on your feet, you kicked her out the door."

"What?" The word burst from Red. "Boy, do you know what you're saying?" Eldorado Red twisted his head around and stared at Vera, who was looking at him with a shocked expression.

"This little bastard is lying," Red shouted, more to himself than to her. "I don't know why, Vera, but the no-good little bastard is telling a fuckin' lie."

"Lie my ass. Why is mom stuck over in Chicago with five kids to feed in a cold-water flat then, if I'm lying? Why ain't she here enjoying this motherfuckin' house with you, instead of raising her kids in a fuckin' dump where she has to fight the goddamn roaches and rats from morning to night?" Buddy glanced out of the corner of his eye to see if what he said had made any impression on the woman. It was the first time he'd ever seen his father really show any kind of affection for one of the women he brought home. If what he guessed was true, that his father actually cared for this woman, there would be no better way to hurt him than to be the cause of their break-up.

"I don't care what lies you say to impress this broad," Buddy yelled as he continued, "but you and I know the real truth, Red. When you got on your fuckin' feet, you left my mother for some young bitch that you probably didn't keep a damn week."

Vera was actually reeling on her feet. She didn't want to believe what she heard, but it sounded as if the young man was telling the truth. She put her hands over her ears and started to flee from the room.

Red reached out and grabbed her arm and pulled her back, and she turned on him in her blind anger. "You told me you didn't have any kids but one. Now I hear about five more kids in Chicago. What can I believe? Is everything you said to me a lie?"

Eldorado Red pulled her to him roughly. He held her against his chest, stoking her hair. He could feel himself trembling as he fought to control his anger. He knew that he had to keep his temper under control or else he would really hurt his own son. "Listen to me, Vera, I love you, and if that love means anything to you, you'll give me the chance to prove to you that this kid is lying. I don't know why he'd want to lie like he's doing, but just about everything he's said is a lie. I can prove it, darling, so just hold on and have faith in me."

"Prove shit," Buddy screamed as he saw the indecision in the woman. "You can tell her anything, I don't care," he said. "It ain't about her no way. I could care less what she believes. What I'm interested in is why you fucked over my mother the way you did. And you're kicking me out."

"You're damn right about that, Buddy. You are out of this house. Now and forever more. I don't think I want to ever even see your lying little ass again!"

"That goes both ways," Buddy yelled back at him, more hurt by Red's words than he wanted to reveal. He had come home to pack his suitcase and move, but now that Red wasn't leaving him any alternative, the thought of leaving the beautiful home was a bitter one.

"Vera," Red said softly, "I don't have any other children but that one there. His brothers and sisters are by other men. His mother left me when he was two years old. She ripped me off for the money I was using to back my numbers with and ran off to Chicago with a pimp in a new Cadillac."

As Buddy tried to interrupt, Red ignored him and took Vera's arm and led her back towards the bedroom. "As I said, honey, I can prove what I'm saying. I've got letters from his mother dating back to the fifties, right after she had run off. In them she speaks of her leaving and how she knew she was wrong. At that time, she wanted to know if I'd accept her back."

"That's a goddamn lie!" Buddy screamed as he followed them towards the bedroom.

Red didn't even bother to answer him; he was too concerned with the woman on his arm. "I even have letters telling me about each one of her pregnancies. It seems as though, after each baby, she always wrote to me and told me about them, and inquired about the chances of our getting together again." Red hesitated, then continued, "For some reason you wouldn't believe, I didn't want her back, more so because she had stolen from me. She seemed to believe that I didn't want her back because of the children she was having since leaving me."

"Those are your kids! You can say what you like! Every time you came to Chicago you stayed with her and knocked her up again," Buddy stated, sounding more like a kid of ten than a grown man.

For the first time since entering the bedroom, Eldorado Red paid some attention to Buddy. "From listening to you, Buddy, I don't know why I didn't notice it before: you're really sick. You need help. You sound as if you really believe those lies yourself." Taking Vera's arm, Red led her to the bed and sat her down. "Even though she took my money when she left, Vera, I still sent her money over the years to take care of this boy here." Red pointed at Buddy. "For fifteen years there wasn't a month when I didn't send her better than one hundred dollars. Some months when she asked for more, and she was always asking, I'd send two hundred. Never more than that, I'll admit that, but always between one to two hundred dollars a month."

"Bullshit! Pure bullshit," Buddy screamed, beside himself with rage. "You ain't never sent Momma no money like that. If you had, she would have told me.

Why else would she be on welfare? There wouldn't have been no reason for us to go hungry at no time if you had sent that kind of money!"

"I was hopin' you'd call me a liar, Buddy," Red stated as he walked over to his dresser and removed a heavy brown envelope from the bottom drawer. "You see, I may be a lot of things, but I ain't no fool. To protect myself in case your mother went downtown to the white folks for child support, I always had personal checks made out to her so that they could be checked and rechecked if it was ever necessary." Red removed the stubs and held them out to Vera. She turned her head away.

"I'm sorry, honey, you don't have to prove nothing to me. I'm just ashamed, Red, that I doubted you in the first place. When you told me, honey, that it wasn't true, I should have taken your word then." She refused to let him put the stubs in her lap. "I mean it, darling, I don't want to see anything. Whatever you say, Red, is the truth as far as I'm concerned."

"Well, not to me," Buddy roared, then tried to snatch the stubs out of Red's hand. The few he got hold of he quickly tore up. Red just stared at him, not bothering to speak. He waited until the younger man was finished, then said quietly, "That won't do any good, Buddy. I can give you the rest of them to tear up, and it still wouldn't do any good. It's on record at my bank, so destroying this shit I've got ain't about nothing." Red waited until the words had reached his son. He noticed the tears running down Buddy's cheeks. For a second Red wondered if the boy's mother had really told him all those lies, turning the child against his father over the years, for no other reason than spite. Human nature was really a funny thing, Red reflected as he thought about the matter. There was no reason in the world for the woman to dislike him. He had never done anything to her but be kind. Yet, she had gone out of her way to turn his only son against him. Why? The question exploded in his mind. Why?

"When you finish packing, Buddy, you can pick up the ownership papers to the car off the front table. I'm giving it to you. Just take it and leave, but be sure to leave my keys to the house on the table, would you? Say we make it a trade, I'm giving you the car for the keys to my own house."

Stung by the happenings of the last few minutes, Buddy jerked his keychain out and snatched the house key off the ring. He tossed it on the floor. "There, I don't want a fuckin' thing of yours. If I had a way to get away from here, I'd give you the motherfuckin' car keys too. I don't want a motherfucking thing you got, Red," he screamed, his voice breaking as he whirled and fled the room.

Vera glanced away from Red; she didn't want to see the hurt in his eyes. She held her arms out to him as he stretched out on the bed. She took him in her arms, offering peace and contentment. He reached out for it with his whole being, embracing her as if his life depended on it. Then he did something he hadn't done since he had been a child—he cried. The sobs came slowly at first. Deep, body-wracking sobs, the only sound a man could make who wasn't used to crying.

"I tried," Red managed to say, "I tried to give him everything his mother couldn't give him."

"I know, honey," she replied softly. "That's where you probably went wrong. You gave him everything he could want. There was nothing left for him to do but ask, and he resented asking." It went deeper than that and Vera knew it. It went back to the years Buddy's mother had spent putting hatred in his heart instead of the love she should have instilled there. But now was not the time to go into something that deep. Now was the time to try and relieve some of the tension that had built up in her man.

Vera kissed him slowly at first, then with more passion until she could feel him respond. Lovemaking was the last thing Red had on his mind, but the slow caresses of his woman began to change his mind. His body reacted even if his mind didn't want to. The sound of Buddy slamming the front door went unnoticed by the two people in the bedroom.

"Honey," Red said softly in her ear, "don't ever leave me, for any reason."

Vera held her man tightly. There was no need for words, each one understood the other completely. Their lives had become as one—what hurt one hurt the other.

COPPER-HEAD CAME out of the phone booth grinning. He climbed behind the steering wheel of the big car. "I told you, old man, it was just a matter of time. That was just our second phone call and we struck pay dirt." He broke out laughing while Tank frowned at him.

"Was that the brick that broke the monkey's back or not?" Tank asked quietly as his partner pulled away from the curb.

"I don't know if it's the final one or not, but it will open the door for us. I found out where our young friend Buddy hangs out. Maybe from there we can get a line on who his street partners are."

"You haven't asked Red yet if we should go all the way if his son happens to be knee-deep in this shit, have you?" Tank asked.

"Naw, ain't no sense rushing it. If we put too much hope on it being this kid, we might just find out we're searching up the wrong tree," Copper-head replied as he picked his way through the traffic.

"You don't believe that shit yourself, Copper-head. We can't be that far wrong. It's the kid, all right. I'll bet you my share on it."

"No thanks, Tank; don't do me no small favors." The men talked seriously back and forth until they reached the east side. Copper-head drove down Mack Street, slowly searching for the Drop-Down poolroom.

"There it is," Tank said excitedly. "It's on your side of the street."

Copper-head nodded in agreement. He pulled out of the way of traffic coming up behind him, waiting until the street was clear on both sides of the street, and then made a U-turn. He parked the large Eldorado in front of the poolroom.

The young men loitering outside the poolroom watched the two well-dressed men get out of the car. Tank stopped in front of two of them. "Hey, brother, have you seen Buddy up this way today?"

The slim, brown-skinned boy in front of Tank curled up his lip and snarled, "Buddy who, man?"

Tank didn't hesitate. "Punk," he growled, and opened his coat so that the boy could see the gun in its holster, "I ain't goin' ask you but one more time, then if you give me some mouth, I'm going to kick the living shit out of you, you understand that?"

"He's asking about the Buddy that runs around with Danny, younger brother," Copper-head said lightly, taking some of the sting out of Tank's words.

The boy smiled slightly, thankful for the help Copper-head had thrown his way. He didn't have any doubt that the heavyset man in front of him with the gun wouldn't back up his words. As he glanced up and down the sidewalk uneasily, his friend standing next to him tried to ease away.

"You take another step, boy, and I'll shine my shoe in your ass," Tank warned the young man.

The kid who had been about to slip away stared back at Tank angrily. He was made out of a little more backbone than his partner. He pushed back his Lord Jesus hair and growled. "I don't know who your dog was last week, mister, but I sure in the fuck ain't your dog this week." Before Tank could react, he continued, "If you're lookin' for a snitch, man, you had better go a little further than here, 'cause you ain't goin' get nothin'…."

Before he could finish, Copper-head went into action. He hit the young kid in the face with the butt of his .38. Blood jumped out of the wound instantly. As the boy fell back up against the wall, Copper-head followed the blow with another one to the head. The boy slumped to the ground.

"Oh, my God," his partner cried as he stared down at his friend. "My God, man, he didn't do nothing to deserve that."

The barrel of Copper-head's gun in his ribs cut off any more words. "I want you to walk over and get in that Cadillac, boy. Now, I don't want to have to repeat myself, kid, so if you don't want to end up like your friend, start moving."

Before the words were out of Copper-head's mouth, the boy had started walking towards the car. Tank opened the car door. "Not in the back, kid, get up front," Tank ordered as he climbed in the back himself.

Even though the action in front of the poolroom had been quiet, men poured out of the building staring at the boy on the ground. Copper-head didn't hurry as he walked around to the front of the car, opened his door and got in.

The huge motor roared as it came alive. Copper-head pulled away from the curb, then made a right turn at the first block. He put his foot down on the gas pedal and the big car leaped ahead. He drove fast, leaving the neighborhood as soon as possible. Neither man bothered to talk to the young boy. He sat in the front seat shaking.

"Listen, brothers," he began, "I don't think I know anything that might help you."

"If you know what's good for you, kid, you had better hope you know something that might help us," Tank stated coldly from the backseat.

As the boy started to tremble, Copper-head spoke up, again taking the sting out of Tank's open threat. "Don't worry, kid, all we want is a little information on Buddy, that's all. We could tell from back there that you knew him 'cause your face kind of lit up when I mentioned his name, you know what I mean?"

The kid nodded his head. "Hey, brother, I really don't know that much about Buddy. I mean, I see him when he comes in the poolroom with Danny sometimes, but I don't know that much about him."

"Just give us the little you know, that's all. Like I know Danny fucks with stuff, but I don't know if Buddy uses. Do you?" The question took the boy by surprise.

"Hey, my man, what gives? Are you guys the fuzz or something? I mean, if you're some kind of mod squad policemen, I'm for real when I tell you I don't know nothing."

Tank leaned forward and rubbed the barrel of his pistol against the kid's neck. "We ain't no kind of police, kid. In fact, if you don't start tellin' it like it is, you're going to wish like hell we were the police."

Without the gun, just the threat coming from Tank would have been enough to start the kid to talking, but the feel of the gun barrel on his neck started a flow of words that even surprised Copper-head.

The boy almost broke down completely. He started to cry, then beg. For a moment, all he could see was the image of his friend being clubbed down to his knees by one of these men. The thought of it happening to him filled him with fear.

"Wait a minute, man, just give me a minute. Don't hurt me. I ain't goin' give you no trouble, please," the boy begged.

"Let's hear it then, kid," Copper-head said quietly

as he pulled up on a side street and parked between
two cars.

The boy glanced out his window, then turned
towards Copper-head. "Hey, man," he cried, "you
asked me did Buddy use—I don't know, honest. I
don't think so. At least I ain't never seen him in no
shootin' gallery. Danny, yes, you know he's a dope
fiend—been one for years. But Buddy, I don't think
so."

"What about the rest of their bunch? Which ones
use, and who do they cop from?" Copper-head
inquired. The boy seemed more inclined to answer his
questions than Tank's.

The kid swallowed, then tried to speak. "Who you
mean, Samson or fatboy? I don't know what the fat
kid's name is—square business, so I can't tell you
that. But as far as Samson using some stuff, that's
dead." The boy glanced over at Copper-head to see if
his words had any weight to them.

"That's the truth, man, I swear. I really don't know
the fat kid's name. If I did, I'd gladly tell you. I done
told you everything else I know, so I wouldn't try to
hold back on something that small."

"Uh huh," Copper-head grunted, "you still ain't
gave us the name of the pusher, or where the pusher
or either of the bunch of them can be found."

Silence fell on the small group in the car. "Man, I
don't know what you guys take me for, but I ain't no
goddamn snitch. Tellin' you that other shit, well, that
ain't about nothing, but when you go to talking about
pushers, that's something else again."

Once again, Tank leaned forward and pressed the gun against the boy's neck. Only this time he used the barrel and tapped it against the boy's head. The blow was kind of hard but it did what he wanted it to do. It released the boy's tongue.

"I can't think of their pusher's name offhand," he began, but another blow to his head refreshed his memory. "Wait a minute, man, I'll tell it to you if I can think of it. It ain't 'cause I don't want to tell you, it's 'cause I don't cop my mess from him. His stuff changes too much for me."

The young boy screwed his face up as if he was trying to think real hard. Suddenly he popped his fingers. "I got it!" he yelled excitedly. "They call him Reno. That's it! A short, light-complexioned guy, that's him."

Copper-head twisted around in his seat and smiled at his partner. "You see, Tank," he began, "I told you the kid was all right. Now, as soon as he shows us where this guy's place is, we're going to give him a few bucks and let him go on his way." To prove his words, Copper-head removed his bankroll. "How much would you say we give the boy, Tank?" he asked quietly as he slowly peeled some small bills off his roll.

As the young boy wet his lips, Copper-head added, "Now, son, all we want is to know where this guy Reno hangs out, or where does Danny stay? Either one will do. If you know both of the answers, why I'd even think seriously of giving you, say, maybe a hundred dollars."

The greed in the boy's eyes was not lost on the men watching him. "Man, for that much money I'd gladly tell you what you want to know. But the truth is, I don't know where Danny stays." As Copper-head stared at him coldly, he added, "I can give you Reno's phone number, but I don't know where he lives."

Suddenly Tank spoke up harshly from the rear of the car. "What's this phone number shit? You can't get no drugs over the phone, so don't come on with no snow job!"

"Naw, man, it's the truth," the boy replied quickly. "Reno delivers his shit. Ain't but a few people allowed to go to his house, and I ain't one of them."

"Uh huh, dig, young blood, don't you fuck around and let us catch you in a bunch of lies now," Copper-head stated coldly. "First you said you didn't cop this punk's shit, now you say you got his number. Okay," Copper-head waved his hand, cutting off his partner's attempt to speak, "I don't care how you do it, blood, just do it. I want you to either show us where this Reno can be found or get on the fuckin' phone and call him and set up a place where you can meet him."

The boy broke out in a sweat. "Now, man, you know that's goin' put me right on the spot. If Reno thinks I set him up, my life ain't goin' be worth a goddamn thing."

"Your life ain't worth nothing now," Tank stated, rubbing the gun against the boy's neck. "If I was to pull this trigger right now, blood, it's the end of you."

The sweat running down the boy's face was plainly visible. Inside the car there arose a smell. For a minute, Copper-head couldn't put his finger on it, but then it rang a bell. It was fear. He could actually smell the fear coming from the young kid. He had heard men speak of it before but this was the first time he had actually experienced it.

Slowly Copper-head picked up the phone in the car and held it out to the boy. "Give me the right number, blood," he ordered.

Young blood didn't hesitate. He pulled out an old, beat-up notebook, fumbled through it for a second, then read a number off to Copper-head.

"I believe we can have Reno meet us right here," Copper-head stated as he held the phone out to the kid. "If this ain't agreeable to him, ask him to let you know where to meet him. Tell him you're driving."

"Man, I'm dead if I don't do what you want and I'm in trouble if I do. Reno is a bad-ass dude, man, he don't take no shit." Suddenly the phone in the kid's hand clicked. He jumped, then spoke, "Reno, is this Reno? Hi, man, this is Carl. You know, Eddie Jackson's young brother."

He waited until he got a reply, then continued. "Hey, Reno, how are you fixed for blades, man? I could use one. I'd give you twenty-five cents for a good one."

Copper-head smiled to himself as he listened to the kid speak about drugs yet never mention the real words. This was one of the ways hustlers spoke about drugs on the phone. To mention the word dope outright on the phone was one of the quickest ways to get a dope pusher to hang up on you. It just wasn't done. Sometimes a square or white kid might come out and ask for some dope on the telephone, but never a black hustler. They just knew better. It was an unwritten law, one that they all obeyed. If an operator was listening, she would have to be hip to understand what the men were talking about.

"Yeah, Reno, I'd like to shave as soon as I possibly could. I got a fancy date tonight, so I want to look my best," Carl stated, holding the phone with both hands to stop from shaking. "Could you meet me up on Mack, or around the corner on Field Street?" Carl asked, glancing over at Copper-head and getting the okay.

He waited a second, then repeated what the man on the other end of the line said. "Good, you're leaving right now, you say? Fine, it shouldn't take but about ten minutes then, right?"

The phone went dead in his ear. He knew the order was in and that the dope would be on its way.

Carl held the receiver out to Copper-head. "I don't know what to say, man, I'm fucked up no matter which way I turn. To think that I started not to come up on the corner tonight, just lay up with my woman, but no, I had to see what was happenin', and now I know. I'm dead. You cold-ass motherfuckers have fucked my life up."

"Did it ever occur to you, Carl," Tank said kindly, "that we might just knock this punk off for you? If we do that, then don't nobody would know you were in on it."

"Aw, man, that wouldn't work. Please, man, I hope

you ain't made me set Reno up for no hit," Carl begged. "That would never work out. Ain't no way Reno goin' leave his house without telling someone who he's going to meet. That way he puts some kind of protection on his own ass. You know what I mean. He'll have to tell his doorman or partner or somebody. I don't know who, but I'm sure he rapped to somebody about where he's going and who he's going to see."

"Yeah, that makes sense," Copper-head stated as he reflected on what the boy had said. "But don't worry about that, kid. We ain't goin' knock this guy off, we're just going to get a little information out of him."

"No way," Carl answered sharply. "Reno is a big boy, man. He ain't goin' tell you nothing."

The two partners laughed, then Tank took it up. "Kid, ain't a man alive who won't talk if the right pressure is put on his ass. Believe that, young blood, and you won't never put too much trust in anybody."

Copper-head peeled off two twenty-dollar bills. "Here, Carl, it ain't a hell of a lot, but it will get you a good fix for tonight. Oh, yeah," he added, "you can buy that twenty-five dollar package Reno is bringing. We'll wait until after you make your buy if you want us to."

Carl's face lit up like a Christmas tree. "You will?" he yelled excitedly. "You mean you'll give me time to make my buy, then get on my way before you move in?"

"Damn!" Copper-head yelled, then turned the key and started up the big motor. "Here I am running my

mouth instead of driving like hell to Field Street!" He
pulled out into the street and burned rubber.

For a brief minute Carl relaxed. "Shit, my man,
Field Street ain't but two damn blocks away. We could
get out and walk and still get there before he'll get
there."

"Well, we don't want to take any chances of miss-
ing our young friend or allowing him to see you climb
out of this rig. He might just know the car, and if he
does, he might have an idea of what we want to see
him about."

"How big is this stud, Carl? I mean, is his name
just ringing or is he really a big man?" Tank asked as
he leaned forward talking in Carl's ear.

Carl hesitated, then spoke up. "He's a young dude,
but he's real sharp, if you know what I mean. He ain't
what you'd call nigger rich, but he's got about ten
people working for him. And he also has some of the
meanest young dudes in the city on his payroll."

"I'll bet," Copper-head stated, then laughed coldly.
The sound of his laughter sent shivers up and down
Carl's back. He knew he wasn't what you'd call a
tough guy, but Carl had never really believed he was
a coward either. For some reason though, these cats
made him shake like a leaf on the tree with the coming of fall. The one he feared most though was the
big man in the backseat. Even though he had seen the
smaller man go to work with deadly swiftness, he
believed he'd get a break out of him, whereas the huge
one didn't seem as if he'd budge an inch.

"What do you guys want with Reno, really? If it

ain't a hit or you ain't robbing him, what's the deal?"

"Where's your brain at, blood?" Tank asked sharply. "We been askin' for Danny all night. We even gave you a choice, either Reno or Danny's whereabouts. We would have preferred Danny's address, then we could have bypassed Reno."

"Say, man, why don't you guys let me do it this way? I'd rather have trouble out of Danny than the real trouble I'm going to have out of Reno after he finds out I set him up for you guys."

"What is this way?" Tank asked quickly.

Carl hesitated as Copper-head turned the corner on Field, then parked on a side street. "Let me approach Reno and ask him myself how I can get in touch with Danny. He'll tell me if he knows 'cause he knows I'm a thoroughbred. He'll just think I want Danny to help me rip off something, that's all."

Copper-head scratched the back of his neck. "I don't know," he began, really undecided on which way to go. It would be the simplest way to find out what they wanted to know. If he could only trust the young boy. But if the kid were to jump in Reno's car and make a run for it, it would only cause problems. And once the word got out that they were looking for Danny, he would go into hiding.

"What do you think about blood's idea, Tank?" he asked, shifting the weight of making the decision off his own shoulders.

It didn't take Tank but a second to knock holes in the idea. Before he even answered, Carl had a feeling the big man would ruin a good idea. It was the only way Carl could see of getting himself off the hook.

He spoke up before Tank could reply. "Listen, brother," he began, staring at Copper-head, trying to make him understand, "this is the only chance I got, man, to come out of this thing without a snitch tag being put on me. I've tried to help you brothers out as much as I can. Now all I ask in return is a little faith in me. I'll get the information for you, I promise."

"Bullshit!" Tank stated harshly. "We got too much big stuff to lose by taking a chance on this punk gettin' away, Copper-head."

"He ain't about to get away," Copper-head stated as he removed his pistol from his shoulder holster and dropped it in his lap. "If I have to, blood, I'll blow your shit out, boy, without battin' an eye."

The implication was clear. Carl had no doubt about whether or not the men would kill him. It was written all over them. They were hired killers. The thought exploded in his mind. As Carl tried to figure out a way to escape, Reno's Caddie turned the corner. The man parked two car lengths down.

Copper-head released the lock button. "Okay, kid, get out and earn your money," he stated as he glanced over at his partner and smiled.

As soon as Carl got out, Tank got out behind him. Copper-head started the big car's motor and pulled away from the curb. He drove up next to Reno's car and stopped, blocking the dope man in.

Carl, who had been leaning in the car window

transacting the business, glanced up. Before the terrified boy could react, Tank came up behind him and placed his gun in the small of his back.

At the sound of the car pulling up beside him, Reno had gone into action. Copper-head had smiled over at him and Reno cocked the small derringer he had pulled out of his pants. He had pushed the button to let his automatic window down, but the sneer on his lips had disappeared when he noticed the pistol the driver of the Eldorado was holding. The barrel of the gun was pointed right at him. Reno let his arm drop back into his lap.

"If you like living, you'll forget about whatever it is you might have down there," Copper-head ordered.

Damn! Reno cursed under his breath. Boxed in just like a silly schoolkid! Reno let his cold stare fall on Carl. "I won't forget this, punk," he stated, trying to make his voice sound as hard as he could.

Carl knew that Reno wouldn't forget. He hung his head down, with nothing to say. He had set Reno up, but there hadn't been any other choice. "Man, it ain't what you think," Carl managed to say. "They just want to talk, that's all."

"That's right," Tank stated as he pointed his pistol at Reno. "Now you just climb out of there like a good boy, Reno, and get in the car sittin' beside you. Don't give us no trouble, man, and you won't have any." Seeing the doubt in the man's face, Tank continued. "No bullshit, kid, just do like we ask. This ain't no stickup, don't worry about that. We don't want your money; we just want to talk to you for a few minutes, then you can be on your way."

Reno stared hard at the man. He really wanted to believe him. If it wasn't a stickup, he reasoned, then he didn't have anything to fear. He hadn't put shit on anyone lately that he could think of, so maybe the guys were telling the truth.

"That's right," Carl said quickly, also wanting to believe the men were telling the truth. After all, all they had wanted from him was some information, so why should it be any different with Reno? "That's all the guys want is some information about that punk Danny," Carl stated quickly, trying to make Reno see that the gunmen didn't really want him.

"Danny, huh?" Reno said as he got out of the car. Yeah, Reno thought, that made sense; Danny had had too much money on him the last time they'd met. Reno smiled as he got out. Maybe that was all he had to do, tell them where that punk was and then he could continue on his way. He had already made one mistake today by coming out of the house with too much money on him. He had over five hundred dollars in his pocket. He seldom came out of the pad with a large bankroll, but he had done it this time without thinking. But if all they wanted was information on Danny, he'd gladly give that up. As long as it didn't cost him anything, he didn't have anything to lose— or so he thought. Reno actually smiled as he climbed into the Eldorado. His initial fears had disappeared.

Copper-head greeted the young man. "Just relax, baby, you ain't got no worry. All we want is a littl' conversation, that's all. I'll bet you thought this was a stickup." At the look of fear that jumped in the younger man's eyes, Copper-head grinned and removed his own bankroll. "Naw, kid, relax," he said as he held up his own money. "See, son, we ain't no drug addicts that need some cash for a fix; we got plenty of that green shit called bread, so just relax. We don't want your money."

As Carl climbed into the back with him, Reno turned away. Whatever happened, he promised himself that he'd still settle up with this punk. He was unaware that he might never again have the chance to settle up with anyone.

12

COPPER-HEAD DROVE around aimlessly while he and Tank attempted to put the two hostages at ease. "All you boys got to do," Tank said, smiling broadly at them, "is relax, 'cause ain't nobody goin' hurt you. Now, Reno, all we want from you is a littl' information on your buddy, Danny."

Reno held up his hand. "Wait a minute, baby, let's get a little understandin' here. Me and Danny ain't buddies. We just do business together, that's all."

"Tell me something," Copper-head asked quietly. "I know you done seen Danny lately. How was he fixed for greenbacks?"

"Shit," Reno sneered, "the cat was loaded, man. I

mean, he was sure-nuff on full."

The fact that Tank had put up his pistol gave Reno
a feeling of well being. He was sure now that all the
two men wanted was information on Danny. If he told
them what they wanted to know, he didn't have to
worry about getting stuck up. He wasn't concerned
about Carl telling anyone that he had snitched on
Danny. Far from telling anyone anything about him,
Carl had his own problems, number one being the fact
that he had been instrumental in putting Reno in the
fix he was in.

"Reno," Copper-head began, glancing over his
shoulder as he spoke to the man, "you seem to be a
big fellow, so ain' no sense in our wasting any of your
time. Let's get down straight with each other. If you
want some bread, man, we'll even toss you out a few
bucks, but what we want is Danny." His voice suddenly went up a notch. "Not tomorrow or the next
day, but right now."

Reno removed a hankie from his pocket and wiped
the sweat off his brow. Even though the air condi-
tioner was on, Reno had started to perspire. "I don't
know the address," Reno replied, deciding that he
wanted to get this shit over with, "but I can show you
guys where Danny and his crowd hangs out. That's
the best I can do." He raised his hand, made a useless gesture, then continued. "I don't like no part of
this shit. I mean it, but since you guys are puttin' out
the muscle, I'm caught in your net." He settled back
in the car seat and gave directions. In another minute
they were parked in front of Tubby's house.

"Well, this is it," Reno stated as he attempted to get out of the car. "All the studs you're lookin' for hang out in the rear of this pad. They fixed up the garage back there so that it looks like a real house." Tank hadn't moved when he'd attempted to move the seat, so Reno continued. "Sometimes they have a bunch of bitches back there with them havin' big fun." Reno tried again but Tank held firm. "Look, man, what else you guys want from me? You asked me to show you where Danny stayed, so okay, this is it. I don't need a ride back to my car, I'll catch a fuckin' cab. Just let me out of this motherfucker. I don't want to know nothin' about what happens between you cats and Danny. You know what I mean? It ain't none of my business, so let's leave it like that. Just let me out of this motherfucker!" Reno's voice was higher than normal.

"Easy, just take it easy," Tank said quietly as he removed his pistol and held it on the top of the seat so that the two men in the back could see it.

"Yeah, baby," Copper-head said softly. "Don't break out in a panic now. We don't know if you bull-shitted us or not, you know what I mean? How the fuck can we be sure that this is really Danny's fuckin' hangout? I mean, we got you, so it would be foolish of us to let you go right now without really checkin' out your story." Copper-head removed his pistol and held it lightly in his hand as he opened the car door and got out. "Now, all of us are going to take a short walk to the rear of this house and check on our boy Danny. If he's there or expected to show up, you guys can be on your way."

Reno didn't like it. The kindness the two gunmen were showing didn't fake him out at all. One look at either one of the gunmen's eyes was enough to warn any man with some common sense. Reno promised himself that he wouldn't wait for their permission to pull up. The first opportunity that presented itself would be taken advantage of.

As the men piled out of the car, Tank made sure that there was no chance of either of the men trying to snatch his pistol from him. He stepped back out of their reach, holding his gun at the ready.

The men walked around the side of the house two abreast, with Copper-head and Tank bringing up the rear. None of the men spoke as they made their way slowly to the rear of the building. Before they reached the garage, Copper-head slipped around in front. He eased up to a window and peeped in. When he turned back and faced his partner, he was smiling.

Reno, constantly on the alert for a chance to make his escape, moved around to the front of the car. When Copper-head turned away from the window, he made his move. He shot past Copper-head like a cannon ball. He moved so fast that he took the two gunmen completely by surprise. Before Copper-head could react, Reno was past him and leaping for the top of the wire fence.

It took Copper-head an instant to move, and then it was almost too late. He could have shot Reno easily as he struggled with the fence. For a brief second Reno had to balance himself on top before finishing his leap. While Copper-head stood undecided as to whether or not he should fire at the fleeing man, Reno disappeared into the darkness of the alley.

"Goddamn it," Tank cursed loudly, "the sonofabitch is getting away."

"Shut up," Copper-head ordered sharply. "You want our pigeons inside to get hip?" He motioned towards the garage door. The occupants apparently hadn't heard the noise outside.

Meanwhile, Carl stood motionless, afraid to run, yet frightened out of his mind by the thought of staying there with the gunmen. The sight of Reno running had almost spurred him on, especially after seeing that they weren't going to shoot. He had started to follow Reno, but he had hesitated too long.

"If by any chance you think you can make it too, be my guest," Tank stated, reading Carl's mind.

"What for? Goddamn, man, you guys done promised me that I could go once you found Danny. Now, I done kept my part of the bargain, so it's up to you to keep yours." Carl glanced from one man to the other. He really believed that they would let him go.

For a moment Copper-head started to let him go. Since Reno had escaped, it didn't really make that much difference anyway because one eyewitness was still alive. Copper-head stared at the younger man. He didn't want to kill unnecessarily, yet he didn't want to leave another man alive who could put him behind bars for the rest of his life.

Seeing his partner's indecision, Tank took command. He walked over to the garage door. "Keep up

with our friend," he stated before raising his foot and
kicking in the wooden door.

Before the men inside the garage could react to the
sudden commotion, Tank was inside the garage holding a pistol in his outstretched hand. He commanded
them to remain still, but that was unnecessary. His
sudden appearance was enough to keep the three men
inside the building staring open-mouthed.

Copper-head entered, pushing Carl in front of him
and grinning broadly. "Surprise, surprise, I'll bet you
guys thought it was the man, didn't you?" he said
good-naturedly. He pushed the door closed with his
foot. "Now, don't you boys look so damn surprised.
You must have expected somebody. After takin' all
that money, you mean to say you didn't think one of
the collectors would be around? Really now, boys,
when you play in the big leagues, you have to think
big, too."

"I told you; I knew it was too good to believe,"
Tubby moaned loudly.

Danny finally came out of the nod he was in long
enough to see what was going on. "We ain't took no
money from nobody," he stated angrily. "Who the
fuck do you mothers think you are, kickin' other people's doors down, talking about some fuckin' money?"

During this time, Samson was looking for an opportunity to make the break he knew they were going to
need. He could feel the pistol pressing against his belt.
Just give me one second, he prayed. There was no
doubt in his mind why the men were there, and he
knew they were there to do more than just talk.

Samson realized that he had been too slow. When Buddy first pulled up in the driveway with the blue Cadillac he should have gotten rid of the fuckin' thing. He blamed the arrival of Copper-head and Tank on Buddy's appearance earlier that day with the late model car. As Samson searched frantically in his mind for a way out, he still couldn't keep his thoughts off Buddy. He was sure that it was all Buddy's fault that they were caught. He was so angry at Buddy that he couldn't think straight.

"What we goin' do?" Tubby cried loudly as he began to shake uncontrollably.

"You guys are going to come up with that money, first of all," Tank ordered sharply. "Now where the hell is it?"

When no one rushed to answer him, he grinned coldly. "Now if you boys want it rough, I believe I can fix you up." Tank walked over to Tubby. Because the man was crying, he had picked the fat man out to be the weak link in the chain.

Using his long index finger, he poked Tubby in the stomach. "Now, boy, I don't want to hurt you if I can get around it," he began, "but if you make me, it's goin' hurt you, fat boy, a hell of a lot worse than it's goin' hurt me, you understand?" Tank then plunged his fist deeply into Tubby's fat stomach. Tubby folded up like a wet balloon. Before he could sink to his knees, Tank caught Tubby under the armpits and held him up.

"Now maybe you can hear me a little better, friend," Tank stated softly as he held onto Tubby.

"Oh, my God," Tubby cried as he regained his wind. He glanced at Samson, then turned away, ashamed to meet his friend's eyes. "I can't speak for nobody else, man, but here's all the money I got in the world," Tubby moaned as he yanked a large roll of money out of his pocket. "Take it, I don't want it, just leave me alone."

Tank took the large roll, glanced at it closely to make sure it was about the right amount, and then smiled brightly as he released Tubby. "Now, you boys had better pay attention to your smart friend here. He done saved himself a lot of trouble, not to mention pain."

"Say, my man, you guys don't need me no more, do you?" Carl asked, creeping slowly towards the door.

When Copper-head looked at him, Carl stopped his edging but continued his begging. "I done everything you guys asked of me, so I think I'll be on my way."

"Nigger, if you take one more fuckin' step towards that door, I'm goin' open your ass up like a ripe tomato," Copper-head stated coldly.

Carl came to a halt immediately. Sweat broke out on his brow. "Man I ain't got nothing to do with this shit. Why don't you guys let me go, please?"

"Shut that crying up, nigger," Tank ordered sharply. He had made up his mind on which man he'd make his next move and didn't want to be distracted.

Without warning, Tank moved swiftly towards Danny and struck out at the smaller man with a fist the size of a football. The blow took Danny by surprise. The next thing he knew, he was picking himself up off the floor. He rubbed his jaw, wondering angrily if it was broken. Tank reached down and clutched the younger man by his collar and, with slow deliberation, slapped the younger man viciously across the face.

"Now, sonny boy, I can play at this game all motherfuckin' night if I have to," Tank warned sharply, "so the best thing for you to do, Danny boy, is to empty out your pockets."

"Hey, man, what a big, bad motherfucker you are," Samson yelled sarcastically. "I'll bet you don't even have no trouble beating up on old women and men, if they happen to be over fifty."

Tank hesitated and glared at the husky young man. The sarcasm didn't escape him and it hurt his pride. He realized at once what the younger man was trying to do, but it still left a rank taste in his mouth. "Don't you worry none, strong man, I'll be over there to check you out personally," Tank threatened coldly.

"I just bet you will, muscles," Samson said, trying to get to the man. "With your partner holding the gun on me, I know you'll just knock yourself out." For a moment the two men locked eyes, neither one wanting to be the first to look away. "I just wish I would have run into you under different circumstances, boy," Samson added, glaring angrily.

"And if we had met under different circumstances, punk, then what?" Tank asked slowly.

"If that had been written in the cards, bully boy, I'd of had the pure pleasure of kicking the mother-

fuckin' shit out of you," Samson said, leaving no
doubt in anyone's mind that he was sincere. The
young man really believed he could take the huge man
they called Tank.

The sound of Copper-head's harsh laughter rang
out. "I believe blood really thinks he can get out on
you, Tank." There was a note of disbelief in Copper-
head's voice. It was hard for him to imagine anyone
in their right mind thinking that they could actually
win out over the huge man. He lit a cigarette and
examined Samson more carefully. Samson was a
miniature Tank, both men being built alike, except that
Samson didn't have Tank's massive size. There was
no doubt that the younger man was powerfully built,
but he was at least seventy-five pounds lighter than
the man he had so boldly challenged.

Tank didn't miss the look of respect his partner
gave Samson, and it only aroused his fury more.
Without another word he smashed his huge fist into
Danny's face. "Goddamn it," he snarled, "I ain't goin'
ask you again, get that shit out of your pocket!"

It didn't take any more punishment to get Danny
to give up his money. He jerked two large rolls of
money out of his pocket and tossed them onto the
floor. "Take it," he screamed, "it's all there!" There
was no trace of the drugs in him now; he had become
completely sober.

As Tubby watched the procedure, he couldn't help
but grin inwardly. He knew he had at least fifteen hundred dollars stashed up at the house. When they had
split up the money, he had taken a huge roll of the

smaller bills and stashed them in his bedroom. Now he prayed that Samson wouldn't try and hold out but just give up his share so that the gunmen would get the hell out of there and leave them alone.

Tank picked up Danny's money and stuck it in his suitcoat pocket. "Now, young blood," Tank said, turning to Samson, "you and me can pick it around about your share of the money. I'm hopin' you make me take it out of your pocket myself."

"Hey, this is swinging," Copper-head said as he walked over to the telephone. "These young bloods really know how to do it!" He picked up the receiver and dialed a number. "What's happenin', Rado Red," he said into the receiver, "you and the chick still swingin'?"

Eldorado Red's voice came back to him sharp and clear. "I know goddamn well you ain't woke me up to inquire about my love life, brother."

"No, you're one hundred percent correct about that, man. We done busted this thing wide open. So far, we've gotten back a little bit more than half the money, and as soon as we catch up with your son, Buddy boy, we'll get the rest of the cash." The sound of Eldorado Red catching his breath made Copper-head smile. He figured it would jolt the old man and he wished he had been there when he broke the news so that he could have seen Red's face.

"My son, you say?" Eldorado asked, having known in the back of his mind that Buddy was involved.

"That's right, Red, your boy. He was the leader of this shit." Before Red could say anything, Copper-head went on. "Now, since we've gotten that covered, I'd like to know, have I got the green light with Buddy? Or do you want us to bring him back to your pad for your personal action?"

"Naw," Red seemed to let the word out. "Just let him go. You say you got the other bread, so just keep that and let Buddy ride out with his. I don't want my son's blood on my hands, Copper-head, you understand? Leave him alone."

It was an order, and as the full significance of the order penetrated his mind, Copper-head smiled. Before he could ask any other questions, the phone went dead. "I'd guess from that that our boss don't want to be disturbed anymore tonight, Tank. He said for us to wrap it up here and it's finished. We ain't got to worry about Buddy boy, wherever that punk might be. He gets to keep his share of the dough, with no problems." Copper-head laughed. "He is sure one lucky nigger, I can tell you that."

"Shit," Tank cursed as he walked over to Samson. "That's money out of our pocket, partner. We were supposed to keep all the bread, so actually it's our money the kid is ridin' out with."

When Copper-head laughed again, it was a cold, chilling sound. "I hadn't thought about it like that, Tank. No indeed, I really hadn't thought about it that way. And as you say, it's really our money." He rubbed his chin thoughtfully. "But on second thought, brother, we had better leave it alone. If the kid should show up before we leave, then it's something else, but if he don't, we ain't goin' go out of our way lookin' for him."

While the two men talked, Samson started to inch his hand closer to the pistol in his belt. It would take just the right kind of break if he was to be lucky enough to take both the gunmen. And that's what he'd have to do if he wanted to stay alive. There could be no mistake when he made his move; it would have to be fast and deadly.

But Carl made the first move. He had talked himself into believing that they wouldn't really shoot. He had witnessed Reno's escape and they hadn't fired on him, so naturally the same thing would take place in his case.

Carl waited until Copper-head was almost completely turned around before making his break. In four quick steps he was at the door, jerking it open. At the sound of his pounding feet, Copper-head whirled around. As Carl went through the door on the run, Copper-head brought his pistol up to bear on the fleeing man's back. The first shot hit him high in the back, the second one was just a little lower. Carl staggered from the impact, regained his balance, took two more steps and fell on his face. He clutched at the bumper of the car. He held on tightly but lost his strength and fell to the ground. He jerked once, and then it was over.

During the commotion Samson decided to make his move. As fast as his hand moved, Tank's moved even faster. He slashed down on the younger man's wrist as he came up clutching the pistol. The gun fell to the floor. Before Samson could reach down and retrieve

it, Tank followed his attack up with a blow to the
stomach. Samson let out a grunt of pain. It was all he
could do to keep from folding up on the floor.

As the two huge men struggled, Danny moved
silently across the floor towards the gun. Tubby
watched them as if they were actors on the stage. He
was too frightened to move. The sight of Carl being
shot down in cold blood had terrified him.

Copper-head stood in the doorway, staring out at
the body. He was undecided as to whether to pull the
body back into the garage or just leave it in the
driveway. He glanced back over his shoulder into the
room just in time to see Danny reaching for the gun.
Copper-head raised his pistol and shot Danny in the
head.

The sound of the shot caused Tank to stop. It took
only a moment for him to see that everything was
under control. Danny was dead, and Tubby stood
shaking like a leaf, with tears running down his fat
cheeks.

Samson took advantage of the brief delay to get his
wind back. When Tank turned around to finish the
fight, he found a far different man waiting for him.
This time it was Samson's turn to take the big man
by surprise. Faking a punch to the head, he buried his
fist in Tank's stomach. Samson followed up with a
blow to the head. He could feel the pain shoot through
his arm. The punch he had thrown was hard enough
to knock two men out, let alone one, but it hadn't
fazed the bigger man. Fear shot through him as Tank
grunted, then grinned at him.

"I thought you was goin' kill me, blood," Tank said softly as he moved in, bent over in a fighter's crouch. Tank's first love was fighting and he was thrilled at the opportunity to engage in it.

Samson watched the man move in on him. This was the first time in his life that he'd fought with a man and had doubts about the outcome. He knew that the outcome of this fight involved his life. They would never let him live. His only chance was to defeat Tank, then try and take the smaller man by surprise.

Samson flinched, then delivered two quick blows to Tank's exposed chin. Neither punch slowed the man up. Moving with the speed of a lightweight, Samson danced back out of Tank's reach, then stepped in and fired a flurry of stinging punches to Tank's face. Blood began to flow from Tank's cut lip, and a small bump appeared over his right eye.

With deadly control Tank faked a blow to Samson's mid-section, then came around with a swift right across the younger man's nose. Blood squirted like water out of a hose.

Samson shook his head. From the pain he realized that his nose had been broken. Terror was alien to him, but it overwhelmed him now. He was terrified by the thought of losing. That fear added to his strength.

As Tank came wading in, he was met by a determined fighter. For the next few minutes, Samson stood toe to toe with Tank. For every blow Tank threw at the younger man, he received three in return. Samson was everywhere, fighting with the blind power of desperation.

Apprehension spread on Copper-head's features as he watched from the sidelines. He had never seen anybody stand up to Tank in this fashion. The blows Samson was landing were taking their toll. Blood ran from Tank's mouth and nose, and there was a cut over his eye. As Copper-head watched, the young fighter stepped in and delivered four quick blows to his partner's exposed face. The punches caused Tank to stagger. Copper-head raised the gun in his hand, then decided against it and let it slip back to his side.

Suddenly Tank changed his style. Furious at himself for letting the young boy last so long, Tank took two more blows to the head as he waited for his opportunity. Finally he caught Samson's arm, holding it by the wrist, and whirled around until his back was against Samson's chest. He held the arm out straight and turned it over so that the palm faced him. Using his forearm as a block, Tank broke Samson's arm quickly and expertly.

The scream that burst from Samson was terrifying. In anguish, the horrified man glanced down and saw the white bone protruding through the skin.

The fight was over; experience had won out over skill. Even though Samson had been the better boxer, it hadn't been enough to win him the fight.

As Samson stood in a state of shock, Tank pulled out his pistol and clubbed the younger man down to his knees. The taste of blood running down his nose only aroused Tank's fury. He reversed the gun in his hand, pulling viciously on the boy's natural and snapping his head up. He waited until he was staring straight into the younger man's face, then raised the gun an inch away from the exposed face and pulled the trigger. The force of the shot ripped half of Samson's face off, killing him instantly.

Before Tubby's shocked mind could absorb what had happened, Copper-head raised his gun and shot the quivering mass of fat.

"You're wasting your bullets shootin' that fat bastard in the stomach," Tank observed as he walked over to Tubby's stretched-out form. The fat man was still alive, holding his guts.

At the approach of the other man, Tubby began to beg. Tank didn't waste any time. He leaned down and put the gun barrel against Tubby's temple and pulled the trigger.

"We better get the fuck out of here," Copper-head said as he walked over to Samson's body and removed a small roll of money from the dead man's pocket. "Sonofabitch, if this is all this bastard's got, we come out on the losing end with him." He searched further in the dead man's pockets until he came up with a car key with a tag on it. The word Cadillac was written on the tag.

"This is where this bastard's share of the money went. He bought a motherfuckin' Cadillac," Copper-head said, his anger apparent from the tone of his voice.

"Well, it's too late for tears now," Tank replied, taking one more quick glance around the roomful of bodies. "Let's leave these fuckin' guns here and get lost," he said, tossing his gun down after wiping it clean.

"That sounds good to me," Copper-head said, wiping his gun off. He tossed it down, then picked up the pistol Samson had carried. "I think I'll take this boy's gun along; it ain't even been fired." He shifted the car keys in his hand, then walked towards the door. "I'm goin' take this boy's Cadillac and follow you over to Red's house so we can drop off his car."

Tank stopped and looked at his partner. "That's cool, man, but I don't see no reason for takin' that boy's gun along. You don't know what he might have used it for. Here we get rid of our pieces 'cause they too hot, then you pick up a motherfuckin' piece that you don't know nothing about."

Tank shrugged his huge shoulders and walked on down the driveway. The back porch light was on and he could see someone peering out of a window. He glanced back at his partner. "I don't think you'd better cut the car lights on until you're halfway out of the driveway. That way, bro, they might not see the kid in the driveway."

The way the body was lying, it was impossible for the people in the house to see it because the car was blocking the view.

"Here, don't forget these," Copper-head said, removing the keys for the Eldorado from his pocket. He tossed them to Tank, then climbed into the blue Cadillac. By the time Tank had reached the street and got into the other car, Copper-head had backed out of the driveway.

The two men hadn't gone a block before the people inside the house came out to see what the bundle lying in their driveway was. After finding the first body, they opened the garage door and saw the rest of it. Before Copper-head had reached Eldorado Red's house, police were running over each other looking for clues to the wholesale murders. A call went out for a powder blue Cadillac.

13

WHEN THE TWO CARS reached Eldorado Red's house, Tank pulled the long red Cadillac he was driving into the driveway and left it. He put the keys in the ashtray, then climbed out grinning. He was feeling good. Their job was done and it had been a clean hit. Except for Reno getting away, there was no one who could point the finger of guilt at them. They had gotten away cleanly. Clean except for that goddamn gun, he thought angrily. "Sonofabitch," Tank cursed. "He'd have to get right on Copper-head's ass and make him get rid of the motherfucker.

Tank climbed into the passenger side of the blue Caddie. "Let's hit a main street and dump this motherfuckin' car," he said as he settled down in the plush car.

Copper-head grinned at him. "Man, what the fuck are you sweating about? It's over, beautifully done. I was thinkin' about driving this motherhubba out to the airport and leavin' it; that way, we can save on cab fare."

"Man, fuck that shit. If we were so concerned about savin', we could have used Red's car and left it at the airport, but not this baby. Hell no, ain't no way I'm going to stay in this fuckin' ride that long. In fact, Copper-head, let's dump this motherfucker right now."

Copper-head laughed. "Come on now, baby, let's not go to trembling. It's all over, so just sit back and relax. Enjoy life, Tank."

Tank cursed. "I don't like it. This is too much like some dumb schoolkid's action, man. We done made our hit, now we're ridin' around in the murdered man's car like a couple of fools. Goddamn it, Head, this is the only thing that can tie us up with that job, man, so let's get us out of this cocksucker before it ends up costin' us our asses."

Finally Copper-head became serious. "I was just bullshittin' you, Tank. I want to get rid of this moth- erfucker too, but ain't no sense us gettin' out on one of these side streets. No tellin' how far we might have to walk before we can find a cab."

Tank settled down for a second, then sat upright. "Fuck it, I don't care how far I have to walk. Let me out; I'll meet you at the airport."

As Copper-head slowed down for a stop sign, he

glanced over at his friend. "You're really serious, ain't you?" Before Tank could answer, both men spotted the black and white police car pull up to the intersection and stop. The police car waited until they had stopped, then pulled in front of them.

"What the fuck's going on?" Tank said in surprise, then cursed. "You still got that fuckin' gun on you, too!"

Copper-head pulled the gun out and kicked it under the seat. The three policemen got out of their car and advanced on them with drawn guns. The officers split up, with one coming to each side of the car.

"Put your hands on the dashboard. Don't either one of you bastards move," the officer ordered in a voice that didn't leave room for doubt. "Now, I want you to come out of there real slow." The officer on Copper-head's side opened the door and held it. The third policeman stood at the rear of the car holding a shotgun on them. Tank was ordered out the same way and brought around the car to stand beside Copper-head.

"May I ask, officer," Tank inquired, "what the fuck-'s going on?"

"We got a call on a blue Cadillac, boy. It was supposed to have been used in a killing. Now, you wouldn't know anything about that, would you?" the officer holding the shotgun asked. He watched Copper-head and Tank while his partners searched the car.

"Oh boy," the cop searching the driver's side yelled as he came up clutching the pistol, "looks like we done struck oil." He removed the car keys and closed the car door.

Tank glared at Copper-head. "You dumb mother-fucker," he mumbled.

The policeman with the car keys walked to the rear and opened the trunk. "Well, I'll be damned, looks like we done really hit the jackpot," the cop said as Buddy's arm flopped out of the trunk. "Is he really dead?" the other cop asked, looking over his partner's shoulder.

"He's as dead as he'll ever be. A bullet hole in his head. Why, I'd even bet money that we got the mur-der gun right here," he said, holding the gun out for all to see. "Yes sir," the cop said, "we got the gun and the gunmen!"

"Gunmen hell," Tank exploded. "I just met this guy. He was coming along and I thumbed him down. Why, we don't even know each other's name," Tank con-tinued, making sure he had Copper-head's eye. That was his story, and he'd go down with it. If there was a way out, he was the only one who stood a chance of walking. He hadn't touched the gun. His prints couldn't be found anywhere.

One of the cops rushed back to the car, calling in for help. As Tank watched him, he mumbled to Copper-head. "Old dude, it's been many a road we been down together, but I can't help you walk down the time they goin' give you, so don't take me along with you. Try to help me walk and I'll do whatever I can to take care of business so well that you won't never need for no money while you're down."

Copper-head glanced at his friend. "Baby, I know what went down. If I can keep you out of it, you're out of it. I don't need your company in the joint. I'd rather see you on the street." The two men's eyes met. They had an understanding, but it had never been tried like this before. This was the big one. When they knocked you out of the box on this one, you stayed out of the box.

"It goin' be rough!" Tank stated, glad that the policemen had left them handcuffed standing beside the car. The officer who had found the body was still standing there gaping, while the officer with the shotgun stood at the front of the car keeping the handcuffed men guarded.

"Let's cut out all the fuckin' yapping," the officer with the shotgun yelled at them.

It was a waste of time. Both men knew that as long as they didn't run, he wouldn't hardly cut loose with the shatter-gun. By the same token, he would stay away from them too, so they continued to whisper under their breath.

"You goin' really try and get out from under it with that hitchhiking shit, huh?" Copper-head asked seriously.

"Why not?" Tank replied, dead serious. "They got to prove it. I ain't left no prints nowhere, ain't no witnesses."

"Shit!" Copper-head stated sharply. "You funnin' yourself, Tank. Ain't no shit that clean. Man, by the time they put this ride back at that garage, them other bodies goin' come up."

"Still ain't no proof," Tank argued, shaking his head in anger. "I ain't left nothin' over at that barn to point nothin' in my direction."

"You forgettin' something real important, Tank," Copper-head stated. "I don't want to knock the props from under you, boy, but face facts. That punk got away from us tonight. He's the key to the whole fuckin' thing."

Tank raised his head and stared at Copper-head. "I see you been giving my chances a close going over. I like that. You and me see the same problem. Without that problem, I can walk. I'm serious, Copper-head. If that young nigger don't take the stand on me, I'm going out the front door."

Copper-head looked away from Tank's eyes. He would try all that was in his power to help Tank out of it, but it was a damn long shot Tank was hoping for.

"I thought my partner told you boys to shut your fuckin' mouths," the officer who had been in the rear with the body stated as he came nearer. His partner, who had gone back to the car, came over too, his blond mustache bristling as he hurried towards the group. He clutched his large .357 magnum in his right hand.

"We better take real good care of these boys. They been havin' a hell of a killin' time all night. Detectives would be right pleased to see them. We even have to wait for another car to join us before we start escorting these gentlemen straight downtown," he informed his partners as he stopped a few feet from the car.

Both of the men were already well subdued, with

their hands cuffed behind their backs. There was not much they could do. Another car pulled up almost immediately after the policemen had spoken.

The officers quickly herded the two men into the rear of the car, then the three officers got in the front. The other police car fell in the rear, then they started their quick trip. They were on the freeway in minutes. When they came off, the officer made a right turn and they were at headquarters.

Neither of the two men had spoken on the ride down, even when the policemen tried to draw them in on some friendly chatter about their whereabouts that night. Both men ignored the silly questioning by the uniformed officers.

Both men knew what lay ahead. The days and nights of questioning. The friendly officer, then the one who threatened to use his fists. The hard iron cots until one got used to it. The waiting, the courtrooms, both of them had paid their dues in the courtrooms. In a way, they knew their way around the courtrooms as well as any lawyer.

But Tank wasn't worried about the coming court fight. He wanted to make it easy by having no witnesses. His mind was busy on that problem. He regretted that he hadn't shot the boy in the back when he started to run. With a dead Reno, he knew they didn't have any kind of case against him. If he could bail out, he could handle it. Force the detectives' hands before they had a chance to put it all together. If he could bail out, he'd take Reno out of the picture immediately. A dead witness was the best kind.

When the two police cars pulled in the garage, there were a dozen detectives standing around waiting. The driver of the car with the prisoners grinned. "It looks like we are bringing in a big catch. All this attention, hell, who knows, it might even help us to get into one of them dress suits every day."

"I don't know if I'd want the job," the officer in the middle stated, lying smoothly. Each of the other policemen knew he was lying because each of them had told the same lie before.

When the police cars came to a halt, Tank stared out the window at the welcoming committee. "Damn, friend," Tank said as he twisted around in the seat, "looks like they really been lookin' for you!"

"They been lookin' for both of you," one of the uniformed officers said as they began to get out. "Now keep your mouths shut until somebody asks you to speak up."

"I'm goin' do just that, honkie!" Copper-head mumbled loudly as he got out of the car. Cameras exploded as the two men were led towards the waiting elevator.

Tank turned his head as newspapermen tried to take their pictures. "Go, damn it!" he growled like an angry beast as he was shoved through their ranks. Many of them stepped back from sheer fear. Strength and a sense of danger was about the big man. People could sense the hidden anger that was inside the man.

And anger it was. He knew now that he could never get out in time. His picture would be all over the city before people were out of bed. As he walked, his agile mind schemed. He didn't have but one chance now. He regretted that he would have to depend on another, but it couldn't be helped. He'd have to reach Eldorado Red. How long would it be before he was allowed to use the phone?

Four well-armed detectives took them off the hands of the uniformed officers. The detectives crowded in the elevator. One of them began to read them their rights. As soon as he finished, Tank began his defense. "I want to use the telephone now. If all this shit you're reading is for real, I want to call my lawyer right this minute. Not tomorrow, but now!"

Copper-head grinned as he listened to Tank. They wasn't goin' get nothin' but dumb nigger action out of Tank. He'd worry them from now on for the phone call, Copper-head reasoned, but what good would it do? Who would Tank want to call so bad. The thought kept worrying him until he came up with the answer. It had to be, he reasoned. Eldorado Red would have to come out of his penthouse and get down and dirty. Tank had the hammer of power over Red's head. If he didn't help Tank, Tank wouldn't help him. By that he'd be letting Red know that his name would be mentioned.

The detectives led them through the booking. Something they never stooped to. They waited patiently while the men were printed, then were made to undress completely.

"Hey, man," Tank called out, not speaking to any one detective. "What's all this shit? What happened to all my rights? Where's the chance to have my

lawyer next to me? He can't come unless I let him
know I'm busted! And for what, I don't even know
that yet."

"Tell him murder whenever you get your chance to
speak to him," a tall redheaded detective yelled back
at him.

"Murder my ass, honkie," Tank hurled at the man.
"You just take your murder and jam it."

"I'm going to jam it, black boy," the detective
snarled. "Right up your black ass!"

"That's the reason you're fuckin' around and won't
let me reach the phone, 'cause you know I'll bail out
of this bullshit you guys are trying to build around
somebody," Tank stated loudly. "I got rights," he continued. "I ain't goin' be railroaded."

"I'll just bet you ain't," the uniformed officer said
as he slowly printed them. The detectives stood
around and waited. When he was finished, they were
led towards the lock-up.

"Hey, man, what about the phone call?" Tank
inquired as they were hustled toward the steel doors.
"If you guys fuck around and lock us up without
allowin' a phone call, you know it's fuckin' with our
rights." He caught their attention with that one.

The leader of the group hesitated, then stated,
"Okay, each one of you will be given five minutes."
Then he led the way to a room and pointed out a
phone to them. "One at a time," he stated.

Tank almost ran to the phone. He noticed one of
the detectives hurrying away. He made his call, dial-
ing quickly. The sound of Red came over the phone.

"Hey, baby," he stated quickly. "This is Tank. We got knocked out of the box. Now dig this. You had better see Reno. He's a young dealer on the east side. Drives a light blue '73 hog. You got to talk to him seriously. If not, well, you know, we facin' all day, Redman, and I don't want to do life in prison, so you take care of business."

The phone went dead in Eldorado's ear. He had got the message. Life was never even and without difficulties. If you didn't shake the boat, you were all right, but let some shit start to slide and it would catch you in the landslide every time.

Vera sat back in the king-sized bed and watched him. She sensed something wrong. "Is it that bad, baby?" she inquired after he hung up.

"It's bad, honey. I have to send a witness on a trip," he stated quietly.

"Oh," she said, and rolled over in the bed. "That shouldn't be all that difficult for you, should it?"

"I don't think so, Vera," he said as he stared down at her, his mind far away. Yes, he could offer the boy money to run, but he'd always come back. It was serious. Tank never would have called from the jail if it hadn't been. He had to protect the two men the best he could. Then, if something went wrong, they would know that he had tried and put some protection on him by remaining silent.

Their conversation had been listened to. From the first moment they had spoken, Red had been sure detectives were on the other line. He'd have to move quick. Red walked out of the bedroom and picked up the telephone in the living room.

"Hello, John-Bee, this is Eldorado Red, brother. Listen, I got work that has to be did before daylight. There's ten grand in it if it's handled right."

"Hey, Red," the voice answered quickly. "I'm more than interested. There's a couple of boys here now that would be more than glad to go to work right now."

"Good then," Red answered, then began to speak. "I want you to find a kid off the east side called Reno. He drives a blue Caddie. Now, if he wasn't able to drive that Caddie come daylight, I'd be real glad. If he wasn't able to ever drive it, I'd be overwhelmed with joy. But it's got to be soon."

"I got the message," Johnnie-Bee answered. "I'll see you in the morning about the bread," he answered and hung up. He nodded to the other two black men, who had been sitting and listening. "You boys heard. It's five grand involved if you're interested."

"Interested!" one of the black men replied. "Shit! For five grand I'd hit you, Johnny-Bee." The men laughed, but Johnnie-Bee knew the man spoke the truth. Five grand was a good price for a hit. And he'd still have five grand for himself.

As Eldorado Red returned to the woman's arms who waited in bed for him, his money went to work.

At the same time, the police department's best detectives were closing their meeting. "What I want you men to do is to be sure to pick this Reno up as soon as possible before he ends up dead," the captain stated and watched the men's faces to see if they really understood.

"Captain," a young detective asked, "we have all heard the telephone conversation, but I just don't see blacks acting that fast. It would take highly organized people to pull off what you're expecting."

"What do you think those were you brought in—punks? Those men are professional killers, and whoever hired them to kill would have other connections also," the captain roared.

As the detectives filed out of the office mumbling, Johnnie-Bee and his friends were already in three different cars searching. They met on Mack an hour later. Johnnie-Bee glanced at the two men as they walked into the restaurant, Mickie and Hi-Pockets, both old niggers in their late thirties.

Mickie was the first to speak as they climbed in the booth. "I think I got hot shit. The dude we're searching for is a big dope man. I got dope fiends lookin' for his car. I promised a bill to some dope fiends if they could locate his car. We can handle it from there."

Johnnie-Bee stared at him coldly. "You think it will jump off?" He glanced at his watch. "It's four-thirty. They ain't got much time." He thought it over for a moment, then added, "He could be anywhere this time of morning. Maybe in some motel with a young bitch. You say he gettin' plenty money, he young, probably likes to fuck a lot."

The three men ordered breakfast and ate it. Still the phone on the back wall hadn't rung. "Maybe we should ride some more ourselves," the tall, dark Hi-Pockets stated. He was a quiet man with the face of a moose.

"Ride!" Mickie repeated. "Can we ride any harder than them dope fiends? They know his hangouts, we don't. I believe this thing will jump off, but we got to have patience," he warned sharply.

The telephone rang before he was finished speaking. He jumped up and went to it, beating the waitress by two feet, as Johnnie-Bee and Hi-Pockets both twisted around and watched. When they saw their man relax against the wall and begin talking, they smiled at each other. It seemed okay. Somebody was calling in about the hundred.

Mickie talked for a while, then quickly hung up. He came back to the table. "That's what we been waitin' for," he stated. "Reno's over at Sportie's after-hours place. If we move fast enough, we'll catch him there. He's strung out at the crap table, so he ain't leavin' soon."

The three men walked up to the cash register and paid their bill. It was just five o'clock. They had time. It took ten minutes to reach Sportie's after-hours place. Though none of the men had been there, they believed they could get in. Mickie met the drug addict who had sold the information. He was young, just eighteen.

"Take me in," Mickie said before handing over the money. "I want to make sure it's him." The junkie dragged his feet and moaned.

"That wasn't part of the deal, brother," he said, looking down at his shoes.

"How do I know this ain't no rip-off?" Mickie

asked.

The junkie glanced up. He realized he wasn't going to get the hundred that easy. "I knew it was going to come up funny," he stated, "but I know Reno's in there, so I'm going to take you in there." He nodded at an old car that held two more junkies. "My friends know that he's in there, too, so let's not start playing games."

Mickie glanced over at the car. "Man, I ain't trying to beat you out of a bill." He flashed a hundred-dollar bill. "It's yours. All you got to do is produce. Show me the brother and it's all yours."

The junkie nodded and led the way down into the after-hours club. Mickie followed patiently. He waited until the doorman opened the door for them and then stepped boldly in. The doorman hardly glanced at them. It was a neighborhood club crowded with youngsters.

The crap game was going on on top of the pool table, which was almost in the middle of the place. The bar was full of young girls waiting for their men to quit gambling and come take them home.

As they stepped to the end of the long horseshoe bar that went around the left wall, the young junkie pointed out the light-skinned gambler. "There he is in the flesh, brother. Now I'd like to see mine in green."

"Which one?" Mickie asked. "The light one with the big white hat?"

"That's him," the junkie replied. "Now it's time I got along, brother."

Mickie nodded, then reached in his pocket and

handed over the money.

He waited inside the place long enough to see that Reno wasn't with his bodyguards. He had a young brown-skinned girl with him that kept leaving the bar, going to the crap game and trying to talk Reno into leaving. Finally, she put on her coat and walked towards the crap game.

Mickie moved at once. This could be it. He hurried outside and waved to his friends. They moved around the blue Cadillac, making sure they were out of sight. As the minutes passed, Mickie wondered if he hadn't judged wrong. Maybe the nigger wouldn't leave. He might send the girl home in a taxi. He glanced at his watch. It was five-thirty. In a little while it would be daybreak.

Suddenly the door opened. From the light, Mickie could see that it wouldn't be hard at all. Reno came out with only the girl. As he approached the car, the three men stepped out. The guns in their hands gave warning. The girl screamed and Reno wished for the last time that he had his hands on a gun. It was over that quick. All three men fired, the girl dropped before Reno did, but when they fell, Johnnie-Bee made sure they were dead. He walked over to both bodies and shot them in the head.

The telephone rang in Eldorado Red's house. He shook the sleep out of his eyes and glanced at the clock. It was six o'clock. He smiled as he picked up the receiver. "Hey, Red," the voice came at him, "I'll be by there to pick up my ten big ones. How about an hour from now? I'd like to have it since that littl' problem of yours has been taken care of."

"Really!" Eldorado exclaimed. He grinned down at the woman who had slept beside him. "The goin' away money will be waitin' on you," he stated casually, then hung up.

"Oh, I see you got that guy to take the trip after all," she inquired.

Eldorado kissed her slowly. "Yeah, honey, he decided it would be best if he went out to the East Coast." He kissed her again, but his mind was far away. He knew that his dues had been paid, once Tank heard about it. He'd know that Eldorado had done all that he could. Now it was up to the white man's courtrooms. At least there wouldn't be a live witness against him, and that was half of the battle.

Six months later, Tank walked out of jail free while his partner went to prison for life. Eldorado Red met him outside the courtroom and gave him an envelope. It contained ten thousand dollars and a plane ticket to New York. Tank smiled. He didn't mind. He knew that one day his phone would ring and Red would be on the line, needing some work done.

Donald Goines
SPECIAL PREVIEW

INNER CITY HOODLUM

This excerpt from Inner City Hoodlum *will introduce you to Johnny Washington, a black teenager in Los Angeles, who knows the freight yards like the back of his hand. He and his pals, Josh and Buddy, hit them often, stealing for a fence. They have to. They're the sole support of their families. But when Josh is killed by a security guard (who gets his brains scattered by Buddy with nunchaku sticks), they are forced to look for other work. They find it with underworld kingpin Elliot Davis. But when Davis recruits Johnny's sister for his stable and later ODs her, Johnny and Buddy come on with a vengeance.*

I

JOHNNY WASHINGTON drove his old Chevy up the steep bank of the Fourth Street exit, turned left and moved down into the deserted, cavernous canyons of downtown Los Angeles. The streets were empty and dark. Everyone had fled the urban center the moment their working day had ended. Very few would dare to stay in the downtown district after dark.

"It's like the whole fuckin' place is ours for the askin'!" Buddy laughed. His large belly shook and his deep black face glistened. Most people looking at Buddy for the first time would have written him off as a teenage fatty, one of those kids who everyone would pick on. But those who knew him better and were able to detect the fact that he carried nunchaku sticks beneath his shirt knew a whole lot better. Johnny Washington knew Buddy's strength and Buddy's desire to inflict harm with that club, and that's why he had him with him every time he went on a job.

"Listen, my man," Johnny replied, turning his gaunt, black face toward Buddy, "this here shit downtown's for the fucking winos, man. We got better shit to hit at the yards." Johnny Washington was tall and lean, and he sat higher than either Buddy or Josh, who was in the backseat. Naturally when the man driving spoke both young men in the car listened.

"Someday? Huh, Johnny, someday?" Josh spoke in a nervous stutter. He was sixteen years old, the youngest of the trio by a year. Short and thin, his future was written in dark, black etchings across his worried face. The streets of Watts had gotten to Josh a long time ago, and no matter how hard he tried to fight back they were taking their toll.

"Yeah, Josh. Someday us three'll be sitting just a little higher. We can't miss. We got the brains, the brawn and the worried man. Now, how could a trio like ours ever blow it?" Johnny spoke through clenched teeth, his cigarette bobbing wildly as he spoke.

"We goin' take this whole fuckin' jiveass town by the fuckin' throat and make it ours! Ain' no doubt in my mind 'bout that, Johnny! No doubt!"

Johnny glanced across at his young companion, remembering the days when the neighborhood kids had picked on the poor little fat boy and ridiculed him in public. Buddy had had nowhere to turn until Johnny came along and taught him all he knew about street fighting, and especially about the use of the deadly nunchaku. Two long wooden sticks, the nunchaku if handled properly could penetrate a man's skull in one swift motion. Buddy had learned to use the instrument of death too well. The first time his neighborhood bully had tried to ridicule him, Buddy had violently cracked the six-footer's shoulder blade. The dead silence that followed the surprise beating indicated to everyone that Buddy was not to be teased any more. Johnny Washington had taught the teenager how to earn his self-respect, and Buddy would never forget. Buddy would always be Johnny's man, a loyal and devoted subject to whatever cause Johnny served.

As Johnny thought about Buddy, he noticed a squad car cruising slowly north on Main Street. Quickly, he turned south and passed the two policemen casually. He saw their white, suspicious faces peering at him from the interior of the black and white. He wasn't worried because he knew that, if you gave them the least amount of accessibility, they wouldn't bother you. No cops wanted to stop a group of blacks in the middle of a deserted city late at night for no good reason.

"Motherfuckers!" Buddy cursed under his breath, gripping his sticks tightly.

"Hey, Johnny, they're slowing down, man!" Josh was turned around and peering out the back window.

"Josh, baby," Johnny began, starting to laugh, "if I

had your fucking nerves I would have been fried out by this time! Man, you just got to learn to be cool. Okay?"

"Hey, they made a right turn! Beautiful!" Josh slumped down in his seat, pulled out a pack of Pall Malls and passed the cigarettes around. "Fuckin' way to make a livin'!"

Johnny laughed. "It ain't so bad, man. We just work our way through school, then become astronauts, you dig? We could make a fuckin' mint on those moon rocks…."

The three young men broke up laughing as Johnny turned onto Eighth Street and headed toward Santa Fe Avenue. The downtown district changed immediately from glass enclosed skyscrapers into dingy, decaying hotels and warehouses. Here a few late-night winos staggered along the filthy streets, trying to find their way home. Home to them was normally nothing more than a flea-bitten sleeping bag and cot, the smell of piss and the liquid in the next bottle. Johnny Washington looked at the remnants of what once were men and felt his stomach begin to churn. He thought of his father, sitting at home broke and jobless, and felt the anger boiling in his blood. Suddenly the joking and laughter had fled. Now it was down to the business at hand.

"Josh," Johnny began in a voice that was cold and direct, "you saw how many trains pull into the east side yard this morning?"

"Three. All of 'em from the harbor, too."

"That means we'll have the good shit at the south

end. The fuckin' guard won't even know we've been there till morning."

"Yeah," Buddy replied. "No sweat, my man. No sweat."

They rode in silence along the darkened freight yards of the city of Los Angeles. The huge boxcars waited in silence until they could be pulled up alongside the loading docks and emptied. In them were every variation of consumer goods known to society. Televisions, radios, watches, clothing, calculators, food, cameras..., goods that none of the three young black men's families would ever be able to afford. These were prizes given to the white man for services rendered. Rewards, Johnny thought as he crossed the multiple series of tracks toward the east side, for being white.

Wilbur Mann watched the little television screen go blank. He stared at the test pattern for a moment, then angrily shut the thing off. No more television that night and that meant the little guard shack at the northeast end of the yards would be closing in on the white man until dawn.

"Fucking shit!" Wilbur said aloud, then lifted his large, flabby frame off the stool, ran his hand across his balding head and hitched up his pants. He glanced at the photograph of the naked blonde sprawled spread-eagle on a tiger rug and his mind drifted back to the afternoon when his bitch of a wife had laughed at him.

Wilbur had wanted his heavyset wife to go down

on him, like he had seen the woman doing in the book that Alonzo, the swing-shift guard, had brought to work. The photograph showed a huge black man standing above a young blonde white woman. Both men had teased each other about the size of the black man's cock, but neither had taken their eyes off the picture.

After a sleepless night, churning thoughts of blow jobs and the photograph burning through his brain, Wilbur had awakened with the urge. It had been late afternoon, and his wife had been sitting in front of their new color television set, eating her second bag of potato chips. Wilbur had walked up to her and pulled her against the bulge in his bathrobe.

She had screamed, then had laughed, telling him how ridiculous he looked. She had thought it was all too funny, then had turned back to her chips and her soap opera. Wilbur then went into the bathroom with his girlie magazine and satisfied himself.

Now, as the dark hours of the morning surrounded the little shack, Wilbur cursed. He cursed his wife, he cursed his job and he cursed himself. The paunchy white man was still cursing and mumbling to himself as he pulled on his jacket with the gold security badge and released the catch and checked to make sure there were six cartridges in the barrel of his .38 police special. The feel of the cold steel, the heavy weight of the gun—its very presence—brought him relief. He held the gun in both hands and fondled it, stroking the barrel slowly and lovingly. "Fuck that bitch," Wilbur exclaimed softly. "I got everything I need!"

With that, Wilbur stepped out into the damp Los Angeles morning. He pulled out a Camel and lit it, inhaled deeply, patted his gun and started walking slowly toward the south end of the yard.

Johnny cut the lights as he pulled up between two diesel transports and stopped. The fence loomed ten feet high in front of them, with two feet of barbed wire on top of that.

"Get the trunk, Josh."

Johnny lit a cigarette and waited as Josh scrambled out of the car, opened the trunk and ran toward the fence. The small black teenager held a large, woolen blanket and tossed it across the barbed wire. He then pulled both ends of the blanket down and tied a huge knot to secure it.

"Okay, Buddy, my man. Let's move!"

Buddy and Johnny climbed out of the car and each cupped his hand for Josh. In one lunge, Josh was rolling across the top of the fence and leaping down to the other side. Buddy followed next, then Johnny.

The jungle of boxcars would have presented a problem to anyone unfamiliar with the trains. But Johnny had been looting for three years already and he knew which carriers to hit. The Southern Pacific lines were always the best. Coming out of Long Beach and down from San Francisco they carried imported goods. The watches, radios and cameras were the easiest to handle and brought the most money.

Johnny moved briskly between the boxcars, going more on instinct than anything else until he came to a Southern Pacific car that looked good. The door was facing them, away from the city side of the yard. The car was solid, not a refrigerator and not slatted for livestock.

"This is our baby, men," Johnny said.

"Let's get the fucker...." Buddy whispered as he held his nunchaku between the bolt latch and the frame of the door.

Johnny watched his chubby black friend with amazement. It always astounded him to see Buddy transform into a silent and muscular bull when there was work to be done. The muscles in Buddy's shoulders seemed to emerge magically from beneath his layers of fat. His entire body seemed to solidify into one massive power.

Buddy held each end of his sticks, took a deep and silent breath, then yelled out in a high-pitched scream as he drove all of his energy and concentration into the club. With a solid snap the huge bolt-lock spun off the frame and fell to the dirt.

"You are somethin' else, Buddy," Johnny whispered softly.

"It's nothin'. Just knowin' where to put it at the right time. No sweat." Buddy grinned broadly, his white teeth sparkling against his black skin.

Josh was already up into the car, searching with his flashlight. Buddy and Johnny waited below.

"Hey babies! It's a motherfuckin' gold mine! Watches! Man, this place is crawling with watches!" Josh brought one carton containing a hundred Swiss watches to the edge of the car and proudly showed them to his friends.

"Motherfuck, Sam'll give us a goddamn hundred and fifty for each box!"

"Let's get it on!" Johnny knew what the risks were and knew that they didn't have too much time until the security guard made his hourly pass. If he spotted the Chevy parked between the trucks, he would investigate. They had twenty minutes left to get the boxes out of the car and over the fence.

The three worked silently and with teamwork. Josh piled three boxes into his partners' outstretched arms. Each man ran the boxes to the base of the fence and returned for another load. Johnny figured that they would have enough room in the car for twenty boxes in all.

Alone in the dark jungle of the boxcars, Wilbur Mann felt like a hunter. The strength that had been sapped from his body by too much booze and too much food seemed to return with each step he took. If only that chick in the photograph could see him now, he thought to himself. She would go down on me right away....

But then Wilbur's heart froze. In a flash, he saw two shadowy figures run between the space of the boxcars and disappear. Looters! Nine months ago Wilbur had confronted looters but they had escaped. He had spent the rest of the night trying to replace the boxes and fix the door to make it look as though nothing had ever happened. But not this time, the paunchy guard thought to himself. That shit's all over with.

The hunter returned, holding his .38 and moving quietly between the cars. He crept up to the side of the boxcar where Josh was and waited. He heard the noises of Josh moving the boxes around inside the boxcar. Wilbur cocked his pistol and moved along the edge of the car to the doorway.

"All right, hold it!!!" Wilbur screamed as he leaped in front of the open car.

Josh stood at the edge of the doorway holding a box of Swiss watches in front of him. His eyes bulged at the sight of the white man with the gun pointed at his head.

"You fuckin' littl' nigger boy!" Wilbur felt his hand begin to tremble. He brought up his other hand to steady his grip. "Get down off of there, black boy!"

"Don't shoot, mister! Please, don't shoot!" Josh was shaking wildly. His body was paralyzed with fear as he tried to obey the man's order. But he couldn't move. His nerves had gripped him as tightly as if he were caught in a winch.

"I said," Wilbur continued, feeling his words strongly and gaining confidence at the sight of the trembling youth, "for you to get your fuckin' black ass out of there!"

Josh stared down the barrel of the gun, opened his mouth and tried to speak. But nothing came out. Suddenly, he fell to his knees. He began to cry—hysterical sobs of panic that sounded more like laughter than pain.

Laughter was what Wilbur heard, also. His head

began to spin, and he felt the first rush of madness shoot through his body like adrenalin.

The shot was fired directly into Josh's tear-stained cheek, tearing away the entire left side of his skull. The second shot entered his neck and ripped the muscles and cords out of his body. As his skinny little body flew backward into the dark recesses of the boxcar, Josh's skull and throat were being splattered against the boxes of imported watches.

Buddy and Johnny were standing on opposite sides of the fence when they heard the shots. For a moment neither man knew what to do. Suddenly Buddy turned and ran back into the boxcar jungle. Johnny climbed the fence a moment later and dropped to the other side.

Wilbur stood with his back toward the approaching youth. He held the pistol in both hands and still pointed it at the dismembered body of the black youth inside the boxcar.

Buddy pulled up behind the white man and stopped short. All he could see was the blood and pieces of skull inside the car.

The little guard was at that moment seething with a kind of angry joy at what he had done. For those brief moments, he had come to be the man once again. The kid inside the boxcar was dead, and he, Wilbur Mann, had killed him. The kid was a nigger and that had made it even better. Wilbur felt something at that moment that he had not felt in a long time. He wanted a woman.

The image of the naked woman on his little shack

wall was the last thing that Wilbur Mann would ever see. At that moment Buddy was arcing his nunchaku toward the white man's skull. Wilbur did not even have time to register the shrill, eerie scream before the hard wood struck him.

Buddy knew it was the most powerful thrust he had ever made with his sticks. Every part of him was there, adding to the strength of his swing. The sticks came down directly at the center of the guard's cap, and the sickening sound of the man's skull being crushed turned Buddy's stomach.

"Oh my God!" Johnny ran up at that moment behind Buddy. The nunchaku was embedded in the dead man's skull, and Buddy was struggling to pull it free. Johnny watched in horror, then saw the remains of Josh.

"Josh…Josh…Josh…." Buddy was in a state of shock. With each tug of his stick he cried out the name of his friend. Finally he pulled the stick free and walked slowly toward the boxcar.

"No, Buddy, c'mon. There's nothing more we can do. We got to get out of here, man!" Johnny grabbed Buddy, then turned him around and slapped him twice across the face. "No, man," Johnny said, his voice filled with panic, "we can't do nothing more!"

But Buddy just stared at Johnny, his eyes blank and his mind uncomprehending.

"For Josh, Buddy. We got to get out for Josh. We owe them now, Buddy!"

From the other side of the yard, Johnny could hear the approaching siren. He wondered who could have called the police, since no one was around to hear the shots.

The sound reached Buddy also, and suddenly the cold glaze left his black eyes. He looked around wildly, then grabbed Johnny's arm. "For Josh, Johnny!"

The two youths ran like hunted animals through the maze of cars. They both leaped the fence without regard to the barbed wire on the top. Falling to the ground, bleeding from the multiple stabbing inflicted upon them by the wire, they ran to their car.

As Johnny Washington turned onto Olympic and headed toward Alvarado, he noticed that the back of the car was filled with boxes. There were at least seventeen of them. That, thought Johnny, will pay for Josh's funeral.

They drove in silence to Johnny's home. Immediately after pulling into his parents' garage, Johnny saw the squad car cruising down the street. He let out a sigh, shared a smoke with Buddy, then fell into a heavy, numbed sleep.

2

THE DEPUTY CORONERS were putting what remained of Josh into neat little plastic bags. They sealed each one, then marked them for later identification. The body of Wilbur Mann lay beneath a blanket on a stretcher.

Detective Thomas Baker leaned over the prone figure of the security guard and raised the blanket. The sight of the man's crushed skull hit him hard. "Jesus, I've never seen anything like this!"

"The kids use 'em. They're called nunchaku sticks. Wicked mothers!" Baker turned up and looked at his partner. Detective Jim Spence stood well over six feet, with broad, athletic shoulders and a slim waist. His looming black presence, plus the cold, deadly tone of his voice sent shivers through his white partner's spine.

"Yeah," Baker said as he replaced the blanket. "Fucking barbaric...."

"About as barbaric as the .38 he used on the kid inside the boxcar, Thomas."

Baker followed his partner over to where the coroners were kneeling with their assortment of plastic bags. For some reason he felt more secure with the other white men around him. He knew deep down inside that the killing of the black youth had been uncalled for. But at least the conventional weapons had been used. A gun and its aftermath was something that Baker had seen so many times that he had grown immune to the sight. A man with his head blown off was somehow easier to take than the sight of a man with a crushed skull. And now his black partner, in that cold deep voice nonchalantly telling him the weapon used and where it came from. It made Baker's flesh crawl to think of it.

A white police officer approached Spence. "The boy's name was Josh Newton," he began. "He lived on Alvarado, just south of Fifty-Seventh Street."

Spence took the wallet and thumbed through it quickly. He found the driver's license and pulled it out. "Sixteen years old..., man!"

"Sixteen and running around with a gang of thugs that bash old men's brains in!" Baker was angered. He was upset because the case was not clear-cut enough. He knew the gangs in the ghettos and what they were capable of doing. What bothered him was the fact that a white security guard had brought it down on himself.

"It appears," Spence began, lighting a cigarette, "that the guard shot the kid here first. The kid was unarmed, Tom, and didn't have a damned chance in hell. Whoever did in the guard got up from behind him...after the shooting."

"Yeah, Jim, I know. I guess I must be getting old or something."

Spence regarded his longtime partner for a moment, then patted him on the shoulder. Both men had been working the ghetto for three years. At first, there had been a lot of hatred between them. The white man did not trust the black man, especially when the black man was on his own turf. But after a while, Baker had begun to realize that his black partner meant business and had a strong feeling for the law.

"C'mon, man. I'll buy you a cup." Spence led the way back across the tracks and through the boxcars. The dawn was breaking over Los Angeles, and both men were relieved to see the light appearing. It had been a long and grisly night, the kind that wore Spence down and brought forth a paranoia in Baker that was sometimes frightening. They were both relieved that it was over.

Spence drove quickly to the all-night coffee shop on Figueroa. The tired detectives ambled inside and took their regular booth. They both ordered coffee and waited until the old, weatherbeaten waitress brought it before speaking.

"Shit, Jim," Baker began. "I've been through this before, you know? Some kids get together, loot, get shot and that's that. We try to protect it, to keep it from happening, but it's impossible. Those fucking kids won't learn."

Spence watched his partner as he spoke. The man's face was pale, and his blue eyes almost washed. Spence knew that Baker felt uncomfortable down here. At the moment, Baker was the only white man in the coffee shop, and Spence knew that he was uptight about it.

"Listen, man," Spence began, "we got our jobs to do and we can't let things get in our way. I mean, there's a fuckin' reason why this shit comes down in the ghetto more than it does in the suburbs. There's people down here, blacks pushing the powder and hustling the chicks and using their own people to pad their damned pockets. Those are the dudes we got to nail."

"How? By working on a bunch of teenage gangs? We're not even close."

"I know, man. It's bad." Spence looked around him at the black faces, living in a black world, and once again felt the bitterness of his inability to break it down. The men upstairs, the city bosses, were more worried about their fucking merchandise than they were about the kids in the ghettos.

The looting of a train, the robbery of a dime store, those were the kinds of things that Spence and Baker always seemed to find themselves hooked up with. While they searched the city for a bunch of young punks, the real men, the syndicate people, were walking around stone free. It was always that way, and Spence hated it.

Coming out of his own thoughts, Spence smiled bitterly at his partner. "Drink up and we'll go file this thing away. It's one for one, and that's probably as far as it'll go. By tomorrow, we'll be trackin' some loser who steals televisions."

Baker laughed. He knew that Spence was right. There were just too many killings and beatings to worry about. You could never get a dead man back, but you could retrieve a stolen television set.

"Gentlemen, I want you to listen very carefully...." Detective Sergeant Louis Bellison chomped down hard on his cigar and stared directly at the two men sitting in front of him. "We're going in after this one, and you two are going to handle it."

Spence felt himself suddenly come awake. This was a chance, a way of getting down in there and trying. It had been a long time since the opportunity had presented itself.

"Now," Bellison continued, easing his bulky frame onto the edge of the desk, "the yard people, the shippers and freighters are blasting about this one. They want the man who did it. Already they've had twelve guys quit on 'em, and that's bad for business. I spoke with the mayor this morning and he demanded us to break it open."

Spence glanced at his partner and saw the tension in his face. His jaws were clenched and he was gripping his thighs tightly.

Bellison moved off the desk and walked across the room toward the city map. In red pencil he drew a square, one point of which began at the railroad yard. "Now, the kid who was killed there came from around here. Considering his age, they got to be a neighborhood gang. I want all of this area between here and here checked out."

Spence almost had to laugh. The man was telling them to search the entire district of Watts. The underground down there would be hard enough to penetrate as it was, but with the area he wanted, it would be impossible.

"We'll start with the Newton kid and work from there." Baker spoke quickly, sitting on the edge of his chair.

"Fine, get his parents to tell you everything they know about his friends, what he does...or did."

Bellison looked from man to man. He was intense and he was shaken. The murder that morning had caused more than one reaction from men higher up in the institution than himself.

"Now, we got a reign of terror that the newspapers and media will latch onto if they can. Get those little bastards and let's put a stop to this!"

"Right, sir!" Baker stood up erect and walked out of the room. Spence nodded to the sergeant and followed his partner out into the hallway. They finally met again at the elevator.

"We got it, didn't we?" Baker said.

"Yeah, we got a chance now. We got a little freedom, a little bit of space to move."

Baker looked at Spence, at the man's cold, brown eyes and his chiseled face. He saw determination there, and forcefulness. They were qualities that he wished his partner did not possess. "You're not after the fuckin' kids at all, are you?"

The elevator doors opened and Spence walked into the cubicle. As Baker entered, Spence smiled at him ruthlessly. "Tom, you got more insight than you deserve!"

As the doors closed, the two detectives began laughing, one a little more nervously than the other.

3

THE GRAY, EARLY MORNING sunlight was streaking through the wooden slats of the dilapidated garage. It was a cold, cloudy morning; a damp chill hung in the air like a sodden blanket.

Johnny Washington tried to stop himself from shivering. He had never been as cold as he was now. His entire body seemed to be without blood or flesh. His legs were numb and his breathing strained. He stretched his lanky frame outward, pushing his feet against the floorboard and trying to get the circulation moving again. Reaching for the cigarettes on the dashboard, he felt a twinge of pain in his arm and found himself shaking as he put the match to the tip.

Then the events of just a few hours ago began pouring through his exhausted brain in a flood of nightmare images. The security guard lying face down with his skull shattered, the remains of his longtime friend Josh splattered throughout the cold and dark boxcar..., the images had been with Johnny throughout his troubled sleep. But then, at least, he was able to tell himself that it had been only a dream.

"Buddy! Wake up, man. We got things to take care of!"

Buddy opened his eyes and, before saying anything, reached for a pack of cigarettes. He lit one, then inhaled deeply, feeling the warming smoke invade his deadened limbs.

"Oh man!" Buddy said, his voice hoarse and strained. "I need somethin'..., like a drink. Your pop got anything inside the house?"

"No. He takes the juice to bed with him, keeps it right there under the covers."

"That's shit, Johnny. The whole fuckin' night's shit!"

"Yeah, but we got to get movin' with this stuff. You know they're going to be coming after someone down here, and they probably found out where Josh lived so they'll be all over the place." Johnny took a long drag on his smoke before continuing. "We'll take this stuff to Sam's before it gets really hot. After that, we'll decide what to do."

"Why'd that motherfucker shoot Josh? I mean, Josh wasn't about to hurt no one!" Buddy's voice cracked as he spoke. The emotion surprised Johnny because he had always thought of Buddy as cold and heart-less. Obviously, there was a lot more to his friend than he could see.

"No need to answer that one, Buddy. Those white motherfuckin' honkies don't need no excuses." Johnny started the engine with a roar. The anger that had been so long in coming was finally surging through him. "But at least," Johnny continued as he backed out of the garage, "at least they're all scared shitless. Every one of them fuckin' honkie guards is probably shakin' in their goddamned boots!"

As Johnny turned onto Alvarado, he glanced over at Buddy. The bulky black youth was staring straight ahead, not seeing, and with his jaws tightly clenched. The rage and the anger were evident.

"Listen, Buddy," Johnny began soothingly, seeing that his friend was rapidly approaching his boiling point, "we'll take care of this shit, get ourselves out of sight, then sit down and discuss matters. Keep your-self cool and we'll work something out. All right?"

"Yeah, I dig where you're coming from, Johnny. But it's fucking hard to keep it easy."

They reached Compton Boulevard and Johnny turned into an alleyway behind the 209 Club. The alleyway was deserted as it was still too early in the morning for street action to begin. In another hour or so the pimps and their girls would be coming out try-ing to pick up on the white businessmen taking an early lunch break. The junkies would be doing life-or-death battle for their first score of the day, and busi-ness would go on as usual on the ghetto street.

Johnny stopped the car behind an old, rotting building next to the 209 Club. He honked the horn once,
then watched the greasy, dusty window for some kind
of movement. Soon the curtain was pulled back and
the moony, black face of Sam appeared. The old man
nodded once and left the window.

"You wait here, Buddy. I'll rap with Sam and get
us some breakfast money." As Johnny left the car, he
glanced back at Buddy. The stocky boy was sitting
straight, staring ahead and not moving.

"You okay, my man?" Johnny asked, leaning in
through the window.

Buddy turned toward the driver's side, stared at
Johnny as though he didn't know him, and nodded
that he was okay. Johnny didn't believe it. He could
see the coldness, the deep churning within his friend.
He was beginning to worry about Buddy's ability to
handle the events of the night before.

Johnny stood at the door and waited for Sam. His
mind was racing toward the possibilities of the meeting. If Sam had already heard about the killings at the
yard, he would try to get the price down as low as he
could for the watches. In that case, Johnny decided,
he would have to go with the chubby, brown-com-
plexioned man for one reason—there was no one else
he could unload the stuff on without raising suspicion.

Finally the door opened and Sam stood there grinning his huge silly grin. "Hey, baby! Wa's happenin'?"

"Got some shit for you, Sam. Watches, over fifteen
hundred of 'em." Johnny watched the older man carefully, trying to detect some flickering of knowledge

in the man's face. But Sam just stood there, smiling.

"That many, eh? Not bad for a young dude like yourself, baby. Lemme have a look…." And with that, Sam pushed by Johnny and walked over to the car. Johnny followed, noticing that Sam stopped when he saw Buddy sitting in the front seat. Johnny knew that Sam didn't like having the quick-tempered young black around when he did business.

Sam's game was selling watches in the lots of supermarkets around town, shuffling up to the white customers, pulling back his sleeves and revealing his watch-studded arms. It wasn't a bad way to make a few bucks, but it was soft, and Sam, with his bald head and his rotund physique, was naturally built for soft work. Buddy's coldness and size shook the little man, and everyone knew it.

"Open the trunk, Johnny. Le's see wha's happenin' here."

Johnny got the keys from the ignition and opened the trunk. There were at least ten boxes stacked inside. Quickly, Johnny ripped one open and unwrapped an inexpensive yet pretty Swiss watch. Sam took the watch and fondled it, then turned it over and over in his hands.

"Cheap shit, Johnny. This stuff's worth 'bout two bucks on the market…."

Johnny watched the little man and felt himself growing angry. His fists were clenching and unclenching. Josh was dead because of these watches, and this cheap little bastard was telling them how cheap the merchandise was.

"Give you, say, five hundred cold cash." Sam stepped back and waited for Johnny to respond.

"A thou', my man, and you'll have a deal."

"Bullshit! Ain' nowhere else you goin' take this shit but here. Either take what I'm givin' or go someplace else…, if you can." Sam wore his complacent smile, the one that most aggravated Johnny. He had seen it on his father during those times when the bottle was nearly empty and the old, beaten man would begin talking about the end.

Johnny thought for a moment and remembered his promise to himself. There was no way out now. Both he and Buddy would have to get off the streets. There was no doubt that word would be out soon enough and they, along with the watches, would be hot as hell.

"Okay…, let's move it out of here."

After they finished unloading the car, dumping the boxes inside Sam's spacious, rotting apartment, the older black man pulled out five one-hundred-dollar bills and handed them to Johnny.

"When's the next shit coming?" Sam asked.

"Don't know, Sam. Maybe in a week."

"Try for some cameras, Johnny. That stuff goes down real good…."

Johnny looked silently at Sam, then turned on his heels and walked out of the room. He knew at that moment that it would be the last time he would ever deal with this little, soft black man. From here on out, thought Johnny, things are going to be different. The fuckin' scene has ended, and there's no place to go but up. A wave of relief flowed through the young black as he took his seat in the car and waited for Buddy. He had always hated this little shit deal, and now, because of what had happened last night, he was out of it forever.

There was no way he or Buddy could ever go back to the yards and deal with people like Sam. It had been good for a few years, providing Johnny with a means of laying some money on his parents and keeping his little sister in school. For Buddy, it had meant that his mother was eating.

But now they were men, and they had killed. The rail yards would be for other young blacks coming up, trying to etch themselves a place in the jungle. Johnny realized as he drove down the alley that he and Buddy had graduated the night before.

SPECIAL PREVIEW SECTION FEATURE

Johnny Washington, a black teenager in Los Angeles, knows the freight yards like the back of his hand. He and his pals, Josh and Buddy, hit them often, stealing for a fence. They have to. They're the sole support of their families. But when Josh is killed by a security guard (who gets his brains scattered by Buddy with nunchaku sticks), they are forced to look for other work. They find it with underworld kingpin Elliot Davis. But when Davis recruits Johnny's sister for his stable and later ODs her, Johnny and Buddy come on with a vengeance.

INCLUDES SPECIAL PREVIEW SECTION

#1 AMERICA'S BEST SELLING BLACK AUTHOR

Donald Goines

SMACK, MONEY AND MURDER IN THE
BLACK CESSPOOL OF LOS ANGELES

INNER CITY HOODLUM